'Kalki' R. Krishnamurthy was born in 1899 in Puttamangaiam village, Tamil Nadu. He was educated at the village school and at National College School, Tiruchirapalli. He was an ardent supporter of the nationalist movement, and was imprisoned several times for this cause.

Kalki was a pioneer of modern Tamil literature, and a major literary figure in his own lifetime. A prolific writer, he is best known for his historical fiction in Tamil, a genre in which he remains unsurpassed. His works include *Alai Osai*, *Ponniyin Selvan* and *Sivakamiyin Sapatham*. He was a journalist throughout his life and wrote for the Tamil weekly *Ananda Vikatan*, and later his own nationalist weekly *Kalki*, on a large variety of topics.

He died in 1954.

\* \* \*

Gowri Ramnarayan, Kalki's granddaughter, was educated in Hyderabad and Chennai and has been a teacher of English and music. She is currently a Special Correspondent with *The Hindu*. She has written several books for children including *Abu's World*, *Abu's World Again* and *Past Forward*. She has also published translations of plays.

She lives in Chennai with her husband and two children.

# Kalki : Selected Stories

## Translated by Gowri Ramnarayan

PENGUIN BOOKS

Penguin Books India (P) Ltd., 11 Community Centre, Panchsheel Park,
New Delhi 110 017, India
Penguin Books Ltd., 80 Strand, London WC2R 0RL, UK
Penguin Putnam Inc., 375 Hudson Street, New York, NY 10014, USA
Penguin Books Australia Ltd., 250 Camberwell Road, Camberwell,
Victoria 3124, Australia
Penguin Books Canada Ltd., 10 Alcorn Avenue, Suite 300, Toronto,
Ontario, M4V 3B2, Canada
Penguin Books (NZ) Ltd., Cnr Rosedale and Airborne Roads, Albany,
Auckland, New Zealand
Penguin Books South Africa Pty. Ltd., 24 Sturdee Avenue,
Rosebank 2196, P.O. Box 9, Parklands 2121, South Africa

First published by Penguin Books India 1999

This translation copyright © Gowri Ramnarayan 1999

Cover illustration by Tapas Guha

All rights reserved

10  9  8  7  6  5

Typeset in *Goudy Old Style* by Eleven Arts, Delhi
Made and printed in India by Swapna Printing Works (P) Ltd.

# Contents

# Translator's Acknowledgements

I wish to thank
— V.K. Karthika of Penguin India for believing in this book enough to urge its publication;

— Bhavana K. of Penguin India for working on it with a sense of commitment;

— Mahesh Elkunchwar, Kumar Shahani and Samik Bandyopadhyay for reading the draft and encouraging me by their joyous response to the translated tales, which made me believe that the book may appeal to non-Tamil readers;

— Seetha Ravi, Editor, *Kalki*, who provided me with the photographs and a sample of Kalki's handwriting, as also other material I required from time to time, including out-of-print anthologies from which I drew some of the stories in this book;

— My mother-in-law Rukmini, and parents Anandhi and Ramachandran, for their support in this venture, as in every venture of mine;

— My husband Ramnarayan, who improved it with his editorial inputs and critical suggestions;

— My grandmother Rukmini, now ninety years old, whose vivid recollections of her days with her husband Kalki Krishnamurthy made him so real that when I read his stories, I feel he is narrating them aloud.

# Introduction

'Kalki' R. Krishnamurthy was a pioneer of modern Tamil literature. A fellow-scribe described him as a filmstar among writers, perhaps not in unmixed praise, and certainly with some envy. Today, Kalki is best known for his historical fiction in Tamil, a genre in which he remains unsurpassed. His *Sivakamiyin Sapatham*, *Partiban Kanavu*, and the mammoth *Ponniyin Selvan* recreate for the reader the glorious eras of the Pallavas and the imperial Cholas with their magnificent tradition of art and culture, which are brought to bear on contemporary Tamil self-fashioning. *Alai Osai*, which the author deemed his best work, documents the turbulent decades just before India achieved independence, seen through the eyes of ordinary people who are inevitably affected by the socio-political changes.

Through these novels, serialized in weekly magazines,

Kalki captured the hearts of thousands of Tamils who eagerly awaited the latest installments. Old-timers recall reading the copies they secured on the street on their way home, before they could be grabbed by equally eager members of their families. Many others will tell you that the reading aloud of Kalki's serials by some family elder is an abiding memory of their teenage years.

Kalki was a versatile and prolific writer. He used his writing talent to crusade for several causes, his canvas accommodating a broad, eclectic sweep. He was editor of the Tamil weekly *Ananda Vikatan*, and later of his own eponymous nationalist weekly *Kalki*. In addition, he turned out political essays, reformist propaganda, travelogues, music and dance critiques, film reviews, biographies, scathing satire, humorous essays, songs, poems, a film script or two, and translations, including Mahatma Gandhi's *The Story of My Experiments With Truth*. All his work was characterized by the distinctive stamp of his flowing style, sense of humour and felicitous use of language which enabled him to get his messages across in a striking and original manner without being didactic. His work demonstrates that any theme from economic policy to experiments in education could be explained in clear terms and in easy Tamil. He revelled in polemical and controversial debates on issues political, aesthetic and ideological. Indeed, some of those controversies

in print make fascinating reading today, giving us an insight
into the personalities and issues of those times, and helping
us to understand the past with great immediacy. What amazes
is his unshakeable self-confidence. While he renders due
respect to everyone, he never flinches from disagreeing with
others when occasion demands it.

The same self-assurance made him write under no less
than thirteen pseudonyms at different times in his life, and
for different purposes. Starting as Tumbi and Tamil Teni,
he also wrote as Karnatakam, Langulan, Agastyar, Ra Ki,
Yaman, Vivasayi, Petron, Guhan and Tamil Magan. Kalki
was the name under which he wrote his major works. Why
Kalki? It was thought to be a combination of the initial
syllable of his name (Krishnamurthy is written Ki-
rishnamurthy in Tamil) and that of his first literary guru
Kal-yanasundara Mudaliar, or his wife Kal-yani. (His wife's
name was Rukmini.)

Kalki loved to cultivate the mystery of this pseudonym.
He did once disclose to a persistent interviewer that he had
hit upon Kalki—the name of Lord Vishnu's final avatar for
the destruction of the world—as the best choice for someone
who was singularly resolved to destroy regressive regimes,
and to 'express radical thoughts, take readers into new
directions, and create a new era'!

Born in a poor brahmin family in Puttamangalam village,

Mayuram district, Tamil Nadu, Krishnamurthy's education began in the classes conducted by the teacher who lived next door and to whom he remained a special favourite, continued at the adjacent Manalmedu village, and ended in Tiruchirapalli town. A brilliant academic career at the National College School there was cut short when he boycotted school and courted imprisonment during the Non-Cooperation movement. Jailed for making 'seditious speeches' in 1922, he was to serve two more prison terms as a satyagrahi in 1930 and 1941.

Kalki's induction into journalism was facilitated by his involvement with the freedom struggle. He received his early training in Madras under the eminent Tamil scholar V. Kalyanasundara Mudaliar in his journal *Navasakti*. His writing skills were honed as editor of *Vimochanam*, run by Chakravarti Rajagopalachari at the Gandhi Ashram in Tiruchengodu. Rajaji became his political guru and throughout his life Kalki remained his faithful lieutenant. This was to be a drawback in Kalki's winning acceptance for his creative labours from opposing political camps. The magazine *Kalki* was later to serve as the mouthpiece of Rajaji's often-unpalatable foresight.

It was during his ashram days that Kalki began to contribute to the Tamil weekly *Ananda Vikatan*. Its publisher, S.S. Vasan, recognized Kalki's talent and made him the editor of the magazine. With Vasan's support and encouragement, Kalki was able to make the magazine hugely successful. That was when Kalki began to promote many writers of talent, in different fields, including several women. This became a lifelong trait.

In 1941 Kalki founded a magazine in his own name with the help and cooperation of T. Sadasivam and his wife M.S. Subbulakshmi, the celebrated Carnatic vocalist. In an inspired move, Sadasivam persuaded his wife to sing and act in the film *Savitri*, to raise funds for the magazine. Later, Subbulakshmi was to star in *Meera*, which became a cult film. Kalki wrote the screenplay for the original Tamil version, as well as a few songs which are still favourites with Tamils the world over.

Kalki was lionized for his works of fiction, from the first novel, *Kalvanin Kadali*, to the last, *Amaratara*, which was completed by his daughter after his death with the notes he had left behind. He is also remembered by a smaller group of music aficionados for his critiques of dance and music. Writing under the pen-name Karnatakam, he set standards which are still hard to emulate. He recognized the potential of many artists, including Semmangudi Srinivasa Iyer and D.K. Pattammal, at the very start of their careers. He shared his enjoyment of the music of stalwarts like Veenai Dhanammal and Rajaratnam Pillai. He was unstinting in his praise of T. Balasaraswati's dance performances at a time when dancing was frowned upon by society at large. He welcomed Rukmini Devi's aesthetic approach to Bharatanatyam. However he did not fail to lampoon the idiosyncracies of the musicians of the day, their mutilation of the lyrics in particular, or indulgence in gimmickry without soul. He could flay the audience too for their lack of decorum. He spearheaded the movement in favour of introducing more Tamil compositions into concerts of Carnatic music.

Kalki was not content to remain behind his desk. Beginning with his active promotion of Gandhian tenets, he became an excellent orator, crisp, clear, always full of quips and jokes. He was adept at raising funds and mobilizing resources for many causes, including the construction of a monument to the poet Subramania Bharati in his birthplace Ettayapuram, and the Gandhi Mandapam in Guindy, Madras. Gregarious, sociable and hospitable by nature, he welcomed artists, intellectuals, and the literati to his home. Fellow-writers were always sure of help when they needed it. When Pudumaipittan, a leading Tamil writer died, leaving his wife and daughter destitute, it was Kalki who raised funds, to which he contributed generously himself, to provide them with the financial stability they needed. And this despite the fact that Pudumaipittan had never ceased to attack Kalki, sometimes below the belt. The differences of opinion he had with senior writer Va. Ramaswami at times in no way affected Kalki's regard for his merit as a writer, a regard that he expressed in glowing tributes. His unrestrained praise of C.N. Annadurai after watching a performance of his play and his wholehearted response to Mu. Karunanidhi's rousing dialogues for stage and screen demonstrate that he did not mix aesthetics with politics.

A surprising number of people still remember Kalki, not for his creative achievements alone, but for his personal warmth and goodwill. He was the first writer of Tamil prose to bring his writing to the masses. He evolved a lucid style at a time when it was *de riguer* to write with verbose circumlocution and embellishment. He not only took his prose to the kitchen-bound women of those days, turning them into avid readers, but also converted a legion of readers who had shunned Tamil in favour of English. Whole generations have grown up reading his modern classics. Kalki likewise persuaded several persons who wrote in English to start writing in Tamil.

Many theses, comparative studies, seminars and a detailed biography have examined his contribution to various literary genres and in several spheres of political, social and public life. But he is hardly known to anyone who is not a Tamil. Surprisingly, translators have so far neglected him, perhaps daunted by his highly original style, anchored firmly in his native linguistic and cultural milieu. 'Kalki Tamizh' the critics called it, because it is racy while possessing depth and an instantaneous communicability, unlike anything before or after. There is hardly any conscious craft discernible in his choice of words and images. They seem to spring in a headlong rush, with few breaks between.

Kalki did not strive for linguistic effect. The pressures of journalism meant that he had to write with great speed, and revisions were impossible. Even in his best works, the writer has to sometimes sacrifice terseness and subtlety for easy communication with the largest number of readers. Brevity and verbal economy are not his virtues. No, Kalki did not write for the elite, although several intellectuals and connoisseurs were among his fans. All his writing—fiction and non-fiction—is imbued with a rationalist idealism and a liberal humanism. In his great novels, Kalki made dexterous use of imagery. Its teeming nuances are unconsciously absorbed by the reader, evoking new responses with each re-reading. He presented places and characters with their sensory minutiae intact. Many passages evoke a synaesthetic experience: often he describes events by their sounds alone, but the visual impact is implicit. Olfactory images, too, play a crucial part.

In 1933 Kalki admitted that art for art's sake left him cold. In a reply to a written charge that he preferred propaganda to striving for literary worth, he begins by saying that henceforth he would be motivated by literary concerns alone. This is followed by a glowing description of spring and summer, reminiscent of the classical poet Kalidasa, which somehow turns into an exhortation to all to wear nothing but khadi, as khadi was the most suitable wear in hot months, and indeed for all seasons! Kalki concludes:

> I began my description of the spring season in order to please Tamil litterateurs by avoiding propaganda and offering something of lasting literary value. But it has ended in my trying to prove that homespun is better than (foreign) mill cloth. Therefore, do not expect writings of lasting literary value from me. Expect these from the hundreds and thousands of Tamil writers who will appear hereafter.

Though this analysis is true of Kalki's earliest writing, many of his works have stood the test of time. He is lauded most as a novelist but recent revaluations have focussed on his short stories as well. These short stories have provoked divided literary reactions. To sum up what the critics say, Kalki's short stories defy all the norms and rules of the genre; some of them are too long to be called short stories, some are really abridged novels masquerading as short stories, many of these tales have little plot and less structure, in some the author titillates the reader with a clever denouement, all of them are full of digressions and ramblings, he is too fond of employing a narrator to tell the story.

The charge of plagiarism was also levelled at Kalki by some contemporary writers, associated with the magazine *Manikodi*, in a fairly systematic campaign of vilification. Kalki later admitted that, among his 129 short stories, the themes of some seven or eight are adaptations. In each case the core idea was taken from some external source, but completely Tamilized in milieu and character. Or, as literary critic T.K. Chidambaranatha Mudaliar says in his preface to an anthology of Kalki's short stories, 'The foundation or the frame was taken from elsewhere, but the whole building and the painting were Kalki's own.' One has only to read 'Mayilai Kalai' to recognize this. The original bull may have grazed in an American prairie or English meadow, but the bull in the story could belong to no region but to the lush Cauvery belt where Kalki was born, and whose scenes he would never tire of describing repeatedly in his works, long and short, with undimmed excitement and love.

In his short stories, Kalki does not write for his readers, but chats with them. The tone is that of the oral narrator in the village square, or of a loquacious story-teller at informal post-prandial sessions on the 'tinnai' in front of village houses. One can almost hear the palm-leaf fans swishing in many hands, and stopping in mid-air at tense moments in the tale and see the varying emotions flit across the faces of the listeners. The narrator often meanders into byways, stops at spots which please him, and shows no sense of urgency in taking up the thread of his narration. Irony is a favourite device, irony of varying kinds from the mildly jocular to the bitterly vitriolic. The general air is one of light and hope, leavened by the rare breath of cynicism. In every one of the short stories, it is clear that the author enjoys the telling so much that he prolongs it as long as he dares. He sometimes runs the risk of stretching it too thin. He does leave a message in each, one which he wants to be sure of having conveyed. But Kalki himself is far too much of a connoisseur and aesthete to allow that message to emerge crudely or directly.

To me, two qualities stand out in these tales. The first is the lapidary clarity with which he paints the scene, and the texture, colour and sound he imbues them with, despite the restraint of length. All this seems perfectly simple, straightforward, easy to render into another language. But just when I think I have it in translation, another meaning emerges, which takes me beyond the largely linear narrative. True, Kalki has adopted some of the tricks of Western masters

like O. Henry. You will find them in this collection. But these
devices, like the denouement, are not used to lure the
average reader, as some critics have thought. It is almost as
if he says to himself, I think this is a good trick, let me play
it on the unwary and the know-all, and jolt both out of their
complacency, let me see if they go beyond the obvious to
fathom my real intention in using these techniques and
devices. In some of these stories, at certain moments, both
writer and reader venture into the misty terrain of the
subconscious.

Of course, not all Kalki's stories are equally good. A few
are downright bad and make one wonder why he had them
published. 'The Raja of Rangadurgam' belongs to this
category. There are others like 'Otrai Roja' which interest
one only as Kalki's efforts at playful parody of popular
Western themes and styles. I see in them a lively sense of
mischief. At other times, inspiration simply fails, and the story
coasts dangerously along as weak farce.

The second feature which intrigues me in these tales of
the 'tinnai' has to do with the variety of tones he adopts,
each suitable to the purpose and mood of that particular
story. But underlying that range lies a tension—held very
skilfully between engagement and distance. The authorial
presence can be tantalizing. Sometimes Kalki announces
himself as the real-life writer and journalist; at other times

he assumes the persona of a fictional writer or wayfarer, ready for the ancient mariner who may hold him with an unblinking eye and an unexpected tale. At times, the author stands in for the reader and responds for us.

To Kalki the reader is a comrade, from whom he expects active participation, not a passive listener to be addressed from the podium and taught a thing or two! It is this effort which endears him to his fans and renders unimportant the flaws they may have noted in his art and craft.

Kalki's narrators vary according to the author's will. Some are nondescript; others endowed with a personality that determines the design of the story. Or the author tells you he has gathered his story from numerous sources, filling in the blanks through conjecture, all of which he has put together in coherent order, thus reminding the reader of the journalist's methods even in his creative writing. Kalki has written in the first person as well as in the third, often mixing the two in a narrator-listener grid of a story-within-the-story. There are prefaces and endnotes, introductions and conclusions, digressions and comments. The more he tries to break the illusion of 'reality' by his authorial and other kinds of intrusions, the more he succeeds in making the reader suspend his disbelief.

Though Kalki confessed that he could never write a play, his dialogues are marked by their vividness. His novels offer the best examples of characters revealed through speech, but this skill is amply demonstrated in the short stories too. He is adept at changing voice without warning, and in a way that seems natural. As the tale unfolds, the narrator's third-person indirectness suddenly changes into the direct voice of a character. This is in the manner of the oral narrator who changes his voice and modulation in mid-sentence to distinguish the character he is talking about. This came spontaneously to Kalki, who had absorbed the techniques of live harikatha narration popular in his childhood in the Tanjavur district. Indeed, his first taste of applause came from neighbours in his own agraharam when he imitated the harikatha exponents he had heard in the villages around his home.

Kalki evokes a sense of perspective in many ways. For example, in 'Madatevan's Spring' the jealous lover sees his supposed rival from his garden below. The man stands on top of a hill silhouetted against the setting sun. Distance and height do not diminish the size of the man but accentuate his tall, hefty frame. The author's word-picture indicates that the lover actually sees his rival as the devil incarnate, preparing us for his fury and frustration.

Dream, daydream and fantasy are important motifs in Kalki's writing. An attempt to understand the past, pride in one's heritage and the determination to work towards necessary changes for a better future are perhaps the most important sources of energy in a writer whose multi-faceted genius has rarely been adequately acknowledged outside the Tamil-speaking world.

Gowri Ramnarayan
4 August 1999
Kottivakkam, Chennai.

# THE LETTER

'Kaditamum Kanneerum'
*Ananda Vikatan* (1937)

*A*nnapurani Devi, the founder-principal of the well-known Devi Vidyalaya, was taking her customary evening walk in the big garden around the school. From a bungalow across the road came the strains of the nadaswaram, stirring forgotten memories. The shadow of a momentary disturbance clouded her serene face, like a huge wave that rises above the quiet sea to crash upon a rock on the shore, only to recede as swiftly, so that calmness is restored. The wave's passage left a little water in the hollows of the rock. Tears stood in Annapurani's eyes.

The school's vice-principal, Srimati Savitri, MA, LT, advanced towards her on the garden path. Annapurani Devi wiped her eyes and welcomed her with a smile. The women sat down on a cement slab under the neem tree close by.

A perfect description of Annapurani would say that her hair had greyed through long years of service to women's welfare. The thick waves of silver above her forehead recalled white clouds resting in rows upon mountain peaks. Though her hair had turned white, it seemed impossible that she was over fifty. Had she discovered the secret of eternal youth? Silver-crowned, tranquil of face and dressed always in pure white, Annapurani seemed to be the goddess Saraswati incarnate.

The events of Annapurani's life were well known. The cruel fate of widowhood was hers at nine, before she reached

3

the age of discretion. But her misfortune became a blessing to other unfortunate women. She returned to school, worked to educate herself, and managed to take the BA, LT degree. From then on, she devoted her whole life to the service of women who had been orphaned, widowed in childhood, or spurned by their spouses.

Her body, soul and material wealth were dedicated to Devi Vidyalaya, established to fulfil those goals.

Vice-principal Savitri was a young unmarried woman of twenty-five. Immediately after passing her MA, LT examinations, She had accepted the school job for purely financial considerations. But association with Annapurani Devi had transformed her. She began to wonder if she too should dedicate her life to the service of women.

Sitting down on the cement slab, Savitri said, 'Amma, I had a real problem today with poetry. When we came to the line "Love makes the world go round", Padma asked me, "What kind of love is the poet talking about?" She is a very naughty girl . . . There! You can hear them laughing!'

In another part of the garden, the girls were playing throwball. Their tinkling laughter wafted in with the gentle south wind.

'How did you answer Padma's question?' Annapurani asked.

'I struggled to find an answer. It is obvious that the poet

4

refers to the love between a man and a woman. But how can I explain that to these girls? It is quite difficult to explain such matters to young girls. I still remember how flustered my lecturer in Queen Mary's College became when she had to deal with this verse. Here we have young widows and girls thrown out of their homes by their husbands. How can I talk to them about romantic love?'

Savitri halted in mid-speech. Recalling that Annapurani herself had been a child-widow, she was afraid she had been tactless.

She tried to smooth things over by adding hastily, 'But Amma, honestly, all these things seem to be a kind of madness. Isn't love just an illusion? The useless daydreams of idle poets . . . ?'

'Illusion, is it? Very well. I shall write and convey your views to Dr Srinivasan.'

Annapurani referred to Savitri's impending marriage to Dr Srinivasan. Laughing to hide her confusion, Savitri said, 'Who knows? At the moment it seems very real. But who can say how things will turn out after a couple of years? Never mind that, Amma. This poet says that all good actions in the world are motivated by love. How can that be right? Let us take the example of our Devi Vidyalaya, which is now twenty-five years old. From Kashmir to Kanyakumari, there is no one who is not full of praise for this institution, and for your selfless service. In this case, how can the poet's statement be true?'

'Savitri! I don't know if the poet's words are applicable to all the good deeds done all over the world. But if you think my labours have been of some significance, the poet's words are absolutely true. Love has been the inspiring source of all my efforts.'

'Who can deny that? Your love for the destitute and the downtrodden is well known . . .'

'I don't mean that kind of love. I mean the kind the poet talks about—the love between a man and a woman. If I have done any service, it sprang entirely from that love . . .'

'Ayyo! What do you mean, Amma? Tell me all about it!' said Savitri, her voice trembling with excitement.

Annapurani said, 'There! Do you hear the nadaswaram from the wedding ceremony? The piper is playing the ragam Nattaikurinji so mellifluously! Listening to it I was lost in the past, long before I saw you. Tears filled my eyes as they never had before. Many years ago, Sembonnarkoil Ramaswami played the same raga at a wedding. Those days he was the star nadaswaram player . . .'

'Do you still remember those details? Amma, I heard you were married in very early childhood.'

'I am not talking about my wedding. They got me married when I was six years old. At nine, I became a widow. Those

6

events have not left a trace in my memory. Such early widowhood has its own advantages. Ah, you laugh! But it is true enough. If those events had taken place two or three years later, I would have been scarred for life, as usually happens. Because I was such a little child, they left me untouched.'

Annapurani paused, immersed in her thoughts for a while. Then she continued her story:

'I was referring to my cousin Ambujam's wedding. I was sixteen when she got married. She was two years younger than me. Ambujam was deeply attached to me. I lived in my aunt's house from the day I became a widow. Everyone there loved me dearly and pitied me for my misfortune. My word was law in their household. When Ambujan's marriage was fixed, all the arrangements were made according to my will. It was I who chose the veshti for the bridegroom, the nadaswaram troupe for the function, and decided on the sweets to be served at the feast.

'The night before the wedding, the bridegroom was formally "invited" to the function and the engagement ceremony was performed. I stood in the hall with the women. I noticed that the gem-studded jewel in the bride's plait was about to fall off. I went up to her and fastened it. When I raised my head, I saw that the young man sitting next to the bridegroom had been staring at me. For a moment, my whole

7

body guivered. My heard swam. I was afraid I was going to
swoon. By the grace of God, that didn't happen.

'I yearned to see his face again. I had not even dreamed
that I could feel such a desire. I tried to control my thoughts.
I clenched my teeth, but to no avail. At last, when I did
glance in his direction, he had at that very instant turned
his face away from me. I did not sleep that night.

'Ambujam's wedding went off very well. To outward view,
I continued to be engaged in my tasks. But my mind had
begun to wander in a world of its own.

'Whatever doubts I had were dispelled on the wedding
day. His glances were certainly not accidental. They were
deliberate. I too became aware of my own state of mind.
Some magnetic power drew me to him . . . There! Do you
see the full moon rising in the sky?'

The question made Savitri look up.

'I had seen the full moon many, many times before that
day, but I never saw such beauty in it as on Ambujam's
wedding day. Nor had I been so entranced by the sweet
sounds of the nadaswaram. The fragrance of sandalwood and
jasmine had not given me so much pleasure until then.
Unknown longings rose in my heart. Why can't I comb my
hair and wear flowers as all other girls do? Why can't I use
kumkumam? Or sandal paste?

'On the third day of the wedding, I took Ambujam to

8

where her in-laws were staying. Plaiting Ambujam's hair, the sister-in-law asked the "crucial" questions about the number of jewels the bride had, and how many more were to be made for her! My mind was not on any of this. Snatches of the conversation from the neighbouring room came to my ears. I listened attentively. The voice which spoke seemed to be "his". How pleasant it was! How appealing! He was talking about the plight of child-widows. He quoted from many savants who had condemned such brutal customs. He referred to several books by name. I remember his saying "Read Madhavayya's tale of Muthuminakshi!" At that point one of the others declared, "My dear boy, your eloquence is most convincing. Why don't you yourself marry Annapurani?"

'"Idiots! Fools! All of you! Might as well bang my head against a stone wall as talk to you!" I then heard someone get up and leave the room. It must have been "him".

'In those two or three days I gathered all the information I could about him from the conversations of his family members. He had stood first in the BA examinations in the Madras Presidency. He was much sought-after in marriage, with people ready to offer even five thousand rupees as dowry. Had I really become the object of such a person's affection? I could not believe my own good fortune.

'The bridegroom's mother became unwell on the fourth

9

day of the wedding. To enquire after her, I walked up to the place where the bridegroom's party was lodged. I kept hoping to find "him" there by some chance. I had barely crossed the threshold when I saw him pacing up and down the hall alone. He came towards me with "Whom do you want?" As I stood rooted to the spot, too stunned to reply, he swiftly placed a letter in my hand, and folded my fingers over it so that it would remain unseen. Then he turned and walked away.

'I began to shake like a leaf in a storm. And yet I picked up enough courage to place the letter, very carefully, next to my heart. Then I went in.

'I was hardly myself when I spoke to the bridegroom's mother.

'She looked long and hard at me. "You came to enquire about my health, but what's wrong with you? You look sick."

'"All of a sudden I have a headache," I said and returned home.

'I went straight to my room at the back and lay down upon a mat. Pleading ill health, I stayed there sobbing my heart out in the dark. After that I never saw him—never saw him who looked like a god and took my heart away . . .'

'Ayyo! Why Amma? Whatever did he write in that letter?'

'In the letter? He had poured out his love for me. He was ready to make any sacrifice for me, to meet every opposition from the world. But he did not want to force me

10

in any way. If I loved him, and had the courage to face the world's derision, I was to hold a jasmine flower in my hand either during the nalangu ceremony that evening, or at the marriage procession later. Once I gave him the sign he would make all the necessary arrangements . . .'

'Then why did you lie there crying your heart out, Amma? Didn't you do as he said?'

'No. I didn't. Moreover, since I had hidden myself away, he must have concluded that I did not care for him, that he had wounded my feelings. And the four days' dream of my life came to an end . . .'

'But Amma, why didn't you follow his instructions? I don't understand.'

'Savitri, even today I am ashamed to tell you the reason. I did not read the letter that day. I read it only after a whole year had passed. But during that time I held it many times in my hand and wept over it. So that, finally, when I did read it, more than half of it had been wiped out by my tears.'

'Amma! What are you saying? At that time didn't you . . .'

'Yes, Savitri! It was the shame and grief I felt on the day I got his letter that impelled me to study further to get the BA, LT degree, and to render whatever service I could to womankind. On the day he touched my hand and put a letter into it, I did not know how to read!'

11

The tears which rolled down from Savitri's eyes shone like pearls in the moonlight.

Was the piper merely playing the ragam Kedaragowlai? Or was he pouring out all the sorrows of the world's great epics through his pipe?

# THE POISON CURE

'Vishamandiram'
*Navashakti* (1925)

$\mathcal{M}$an of Faith. That would be the most fitting description of our town's postmaster. The *Bhagavata Purana* was his sacred scripture, and Krishna his God. He had built a small, lovely mandapam in the main room of his home and enshrined Lord Krishna there. Every evening, his wife would decorate the picture with garlands of flowers and light the lamp. The postmaster would tune the tambura and chant the name of Rama. On Saturdays and on Ekadasi, he would conduct group singing of devotional songs. Afterwards, sundal, vadai and payasam were distributed to the delighted children.

Narayana Iyer had no children. But it was as though all the town's children were his own. That, despite his being a teacher by profession! The children were ready to do anything for their 'Sir'. Not out of fear, but because they loved him.

His students knew every tale in the Ramayana, the Mahabharata and the *Bhagavata*. He would announce a prize of sugar-candy for any pupil who could recite three verses from Tayumanavar's hymns. If no one did, he distributed the sugar-candy to all the boys.

For the festive month of Margazhi, Narayana Iyer's wife started gathering together groceries and other materials from Purattasi, two months in advance. At the crack of dawn, the children would go round the town singing bhajans. The procession ended at the postmaster's house. To see the children relish their offerings of puliyodarai and sarkarai pongal made the couple extremely happy.

You may think I exaggerate because I am an old student of his. But you only have to ask anyone within five hundred miles of our town and they will support my words. The postmaster was held in high esteem and wielded tremendous influence in the region.

His influence had nothing to do with money. He did not possess much material wealth. His reputation was founded on the purity of his lifestyle and his piety.

His skill at drawing the poison from snakebite or scorpion-sting through incantations was yet another reason for the respect he commanded from people. At any time of the day or night, if a snakebite victim was brought to him, he would begin the rite without the least hesitation. He would disregard his own state of health—no ailment from headache to malarial fever could stop him. He would plunge into the cold tank, and emerge wrapped in a dripping wet cloth to begin the chant. The poison would drain away from those who had fainted under its impact.

The victims regained consciousness to bless the name of 'Postal Iyer' as they took their leave of him. But Iyer would suffer from blinding migraine for the next two or three days.

Narayana Iyer cherished a great reverence for Mahatma

16

Gandhi. He was a nationalist at heart. After the partition of Bengal, he became a staunch supporter of Swadeshi—goods of Indian manufacture. But the eradication of untouchability propagated by the Gandhian code was something he could never bring himself to accept. There was no end to our arguments on the subject. Having exhausted all the arrows in his quiver, he would deliver a final shot.

'All right. I will prove it before your very eyes. Bring any man bitten by a poisonous serpent to me. He may have swooned as many as three times before coming to me. I can still draw the poison from his body. Many times have you yourself witnessed the power of my chants. However, if even the breeze passing by a pariah blows on me after my purificatory dip, the mantra does not work. The poison cannot be expelled. What do you say to that?'

I had no weapon to counter this Parthian shot. And no one happening to listen to our debates had the least hesitation in deciding in favour of the postmaster.

One day I heard that an Inspector had come to carry out a routine check at the post office. I went there with the idea of indulging in some friendly gossip.

Postal Inspector Pedda Perumal Pillai was a gregarious man. There was nothing unsociable about him. Moreover I perceived he wore an undershirt of khadi. I promptly fell in love with him!

17

The postmaster introduced me to him as a participant in the Non-Cooperation Movement. Somehow the talk veered to the behaviour of government servants in dealing with the public.

'A clerk earning Rs 30 a month, how rude he is when anyone approaches him for some small assistance! How churlish! Go to any post office or railway station in Tamil Nadu and try to extract information out of any employee there. You have to put up with "Get lost!" barked out a hundred times within a single minute. Never do these men realize they are public servants, or that their monthly salaries come from the tax payers. They don't bother to show anyone the respect due to another human being. They never make the mistake of slipping in a pleasant word. When will such attitudes change? When will we realize that an appeal for assistance is a matter of good fortune, an opportunity to help our fellow men?' My gushing eloquence contained all the zeal of the reformer.

'There's much truth in what you say. But there is a reason for the petulance of public servants. Their irritation mostly stems from being overworked. Some do retain their sweet nature despite the workload.'

'Certainly they do! Like our own postmaster here!'

The postmaster intervened to say, 'There are many evils in this country. The only remedy for every one of them is freedom for the nation.'

18

The discussion moved on to related subjects . . . the freedom struggle, Mahatma Gandhi, the Non-Cooperation Movement . . . and finally came to dwell on untouchability.

'Until the curse of untouchability is removed, this land will not achieve independence,' said I with all the force I could muster.

'In that case we must throw our ancient scriptures and sacred texts into the floods. I don't want freedom at that cost!' declared Narayana Iyer.

I looked at Inspector Pedda Perumal Pillai to see which side he would take. For a split second his face was clouded in darkness. But the very next instant, stroking his moustache with his usual smile, he said, 'The postmaster seems to be firmly committed to orthodoxy.'

'I will prove that the outcaste carries contamination,' the postmaster told him. I grew nervous.

With the hope of somehow garnering his support, I asked the Inspector, 'What do you think?'

But he disappointed me with a non-committal statement. 'Oh, I have no opinion at all in this matter.'

Defeat was now certain. I felt very small. Pedda Perumal Pillai turned to the postmaster and asked him, 'You said you could prove that the untouchable was tainted. How will you do that?'

I rushed ahead of the postmaster in my eagerness to reply.

19

I described the power of his spell against poison. I mentioned also the postmaster's conviction that if an outcaste came anywhere near the spot, the spell lost its power. My tone was sceptical, hoping to draw the Inspector into dismissing that belief.

But alas! Even Providence came to aid the postmaster! As soon as I had finished speaking, some four or five men appeared with a victim of snakebite, as if expressly to strengthen the postmaster's case. One of them gasped out, 'Ayyo! Please save him! He has fainted a second time. A huge serpent! The fangs have sunk deep.'

Oh to see Narayana Iyer then! For someone over fifty, ravaged by chronic malarial fever, his poor health making him unsteady as he walked, Iyer displayed the vigour of a twenty-year-old youngster. He sent someone to buy camphor and turmeric, another to collect twenty-one small pebbles.

With the Inspector's permission, he went to ritually immerse himself in the tank across the street. He made arrangements to have untouchables kept away from the area. He returned swiftly to the post office, sat down in his dripping clothes and began to chant. The Inspector sat beside him and watched the proceedings with deep interest.

The postmaster tore a long strip from one side of his upper cloth and dipped it in turmeric-water. He tied the twenty-one pebbles separately into it in a row, one after another. He continued to chant through these operations. The chanting went on for about fifteen minutes. While he chanted, the camphor was kept burning in the middle of a big tray over which sacred ash had been sprinkled.

When the incantation was over, Narayana Iyer got up, took the cloth in which he had tied the pebbles, and put it around the victim's neck like a garland. He knotted the ends. Then he had the sacred ash smeared all over the victim's body. In a few minutes, the man who lay in a dead faint regained consciousness. Within half an hour, he had recovered completely and was able to walk home.

The postmaster looked at us and said, 'By God's grace, I have been able to master this mantra. And so, though I don't possess other means to assist my fellow men, I am still able to help them in this way. But my young friend remains angry with me because I don't oppose untouchability.'

The Inspector broke into a smile. I felt deeply humiliated. I thought of cursing Gandhi.

'I assure you on the basis of a whole lifetime's experience, this mantra has even brought back to life a man who had actually stepped into the other world. But if even the air passing over an outcaste had touched me, or if I had sighted a pariah in the distance, the spell would have been broken. I would have had to immerse myself in water all over again, and perform the whole rite a second time. And so I ask you, how can I believe that the untouchable has no inherent contamination?'

What has happened to Postal Inspector Pedda Perumal Pillai? Why is he roaring with laughter? Is he so delighted with my discomfiture? Or has he suddenly lost his wits?

But very soon we knew the cause of his merriment. I was thunderstruck when he revealed the true reason.

'Narayana Iyer! You were greatly deceived. Forgive me, I am an untouchable.'

We were both too stunned to speak. The Inspector explained in detail:

'It is a long time since I disclosed to anyone the fact that I am an outcaste. I was born in Singapore. My parents died when I was young. Luckily they had saved some money. They had also given me an education. When they died I returned to this country, passed out of college, got myself a job. After that I returned to Singapore only once, to get married. I don't have any relatives here. So far I have not announced to the world that I am a pariah. Nor was there any necessity to do so.'

The postmaster was struck dumb for a while. Then he spoke as if to himself, 'Well, I am very happy to know this! It proves that the untouchable has no inborn taint. I must have misunderstood what my guru said to me. He warned me particularly against the contamination of menstruating

22

women. Perhaps because the untouchable community does not observe this taboo, I think he said that their proximity must be avoided. Since you have led a pure life, your presence did not affect the spell. Anyway, I am now clear in my mind that untouchability has nothing to do with one's birth. My eyes are opened!'

'My eyes too were opened only now,' declared the Inspector. 'Until today I believed there was something inferior about my birth. I was ashamed to say I am an outcaste. But now I have learnt that God has made no distinctions. He has made every man equal. From now on there is no reason for me to hide my origin.'

I broke into song, 'Freedom for the pariahs, the tiyyas and the pulayas . . .'

# THE REBIRTH OF SRIKANTHAN

'Srikanthan Punarjanmam'
*Kalaimagal* (date unknown)

# 1

$S$rikanthan belonged to a well-to-do family. He was indubitably its son, physically as masculine as they come. No,
there was nothing to suggest the girl in him.

Srikanthan's birth coincided with that of the twentieth
century. When the twentieth century reached the year 1931,
Srikanthan too turned thirty-one.

Before we go ahead, let us glance briefly at the history of
Srikanthan and his dear ones in those three decades.

His father Ekambara Iyer had been a zillah munsiff. He
was appointed sub-judge soon after Srikanthan's birth.
Naturally everyone attributed Iyer's promotion to the
auspicious timing of the boy's arrival. When Iyer retired with
many years of work behind him, he was all of fifty-eight years
old, though he was not a day over fifty-five according to
official records. He continues to draw his pension with
unfailing regularity. Not once has he been known to refuse it.

Iyer is a devout performer of religious rituals. Panchami
Ghanapatigal, the town priest, depends entirely on Iyer to meet
the expenses of his daughter's wedding. The enemies of the
priest say he trusts Iyer's funeral rites will fulfil this need.

People who met Srikanthan's mother invariably
announced that she so much resembled Mahalakshmi, the
goddess of Wealth, that the two ladies had to be sisters.

The gracious matriarch was born into a large family of eleven siblings and several cousins. She was responsible for a sizeable increase in the number of members of the household she entered upon her marriage. She had a husband who went daily to court, four daughters married into respectable families, four sons-in-law who cherished them as the eye treasures its spectacles, a brood of grandsons and granddaughters, and many more gifts of good fortune. But she did have one grouse. She had no daughter-in-law to drive the beggar from the door. And whose fault was it? Hadn't they got their son married at the proper time?

Strange that Srikanthan's four sisters should have all been older than him! Their love for him could not be assessed merely by weights and measures. In infancy, not for a single instant was he left untended; later his sisters fought for the privilege of brushing his teeth and dressing his hair. On his wedding day, their fierce competition resulted in all four of them lining his eyes with kohl. Consequently, the eyes which weep for the sufferings of other limbs, were forced to weep for themselves. Even today Srikanthan shudders when he recalls the tortures he endured through his four-day-wedding.

Further delay in describing Srikanthan's wife will stall the story.

Srikanthan was married at the early age of eighteen. His twelve-year-old bride was the youngest daughter of a landowner with five hundred acres to his name. She was the peer of the goddess Rati in the art of weeping. That's right, aren't Rati's wails at the death of her consort Manmatha world-famous? Moreover, no painted divinity on a mural was as fleet of foot as she.

It was not at all surprising that Srikanthan should have lavished incalculable love upon such a wife. In fact, everyone came to know that on their very first night together, the bride and the groom opened their window and trimmed the lamp for their game of cards.

No one knows whose envy or evil eye brought this life of love to a sudden end. Srikanthan's wife was mysteriously afflicted. Some said it was a disease, others called it hysteria. Some believed she was possessed. There were those who talked of the black arts. A few wicked tongues whispered that her mother-in-law had poisoned her. How did it matter? Whatever it was, after two years with her husband, the girl left for her parents' home, never to return. After five or six years of illness, smart girl that she was, she left this sad world forever.

In appearance Srikanthan had much in common with Manmatha, the God of Love. He had the same number of limbs—two legs and two arms—and eyes and nose as the god possessed before he was reduced to ashes. But he differed sharply from the god in character and conduct.

Instead of seeking men and women at eventide, with sugarcane bow and flower arrows, Srikanthan went to the town hall club to play ping-pong. In fact, after his wife's departure from his house, Srikanthan's whole life came to be centred on ping-pong. He became proficient in the game, participated in many tournaments, and won several trophies. These were displayed in neat rows in one of his wedding gifts—a glass showcase.

Srikanthan had graduated and joined the FL course when his wife lost her wits. He gave up his studies then and did not try to get a job. His father brought no pressure to bear on him. He was only too glad to see his son escape heartbreak and lead a normal life.

After the death of his wife, his mother and sisters often pestered him to marry again. But Srikanthan invariably begged them to never raise the subject with him. His grief and obstinacy succeeded in sealing their lips for a while.

However, in 1931, Srikanthan's life was touched by a singular event.

## 2

In the beginning of that year, staunch passive resistance was offered in the town of Srikanthan's birth, upbringing and ping-pong tournaments. The representatives of the government discharged their duties with the stick. They also performed other acts of great valour. They sealed the offices of the Congress party and the rooms occupied by its volunteers. The public was severely warned not to offer food or shelter to Congress workers.

Terror hung over the town for a few days. Every householder locked and bolted the front door as soon as he sighted a white cap in the distance.

The one person in the whole town who possessed manliness enough to defy the state order happened to be a woman. Her name was Srimati Vasundhara Devi.

Appointed principal of a municipal school for women, she had come to live in that town just a few months before the event. She could not have been more than twenty-two years old. She occupied a little house with her aged father. A restaurant delivered their meals. When Vasundhara was at school, the father practised on his old fiddle.

One day, a couple of lean, hungry and well-flogged satyagrahis landed on their doorstep. Even the old man's fiddling could not deter them from slumping down upon her threshold. It was there that Vasundhara found them when she returned from school.

Vasundhara's sympathy had been aroused by the happenings in town. Her heart melted when she actually saw the volunteers face to face. She took them in and fed them their meal from the restaurant.

31

The news spread like wildfire. No one could talk of anything else. It even reached the town hall club and the ping-pong table.

'Courage is essential. That's what I say. Without courage can anyone be counted a human being? She may be a mere woman. But I ask you, does any whiskered male in this town have her guts?' The words fell on Srikanthan's ear, but hardly made any impression on his mind. He took no interest in the matter.

Two weeks later, Srikanthan paid more attention when the same voice mentioned Vasundhara by name. 'Do you know that a big public meeting is to be held today? Vasundhara Devi is going to sing the national song there!'

'An unusual name . . . Is she a Bengali, or perhaps a Gujarati?' Srikanthan enquired.

'That's what is funny about the whole thing. She is a Tamil all right. She has changed her name, but her father is Ramakrishna Iyer. They live in a house by themselves.'

'Really? Why did she change her name? Who are they? Where do they come from?'

'Don't know. Their past is a mystery. Some say she is not yet married. Others say her husband is dead. There are those who claim the husband is alive somewhere. On the whole we can see they have suffered a lot.'

That day Srikanthan attended the public meeting.

32

It was held to celebrate the Gandhi-Irwin accord. The Mahatma had been released from prison the day after Vasundhara ministered to the volunteers. That was the reason official action had not been taken against her. A few days later Mahatma Gandhi and Viceroy Irwin signed a peace treaty. Vasundhara played a central role in all the celebrations held to mark the joyous occasion. Her national song cast a spell of complete silence upon the huge, billowing crowd. It was no wonder that all those who had been ceaselessly discussing and speculating about her should have been struck dumb when they saw her for the first time. Especially when she turned out to be a young woman of beauty, dignity and elegance. Srikanthan was lost in a trance.

No speaker at the meeting failed to mention Vasundhara Devi's courage as a shining example. An exuberant youngster got up and shouted, 'Vasundhara Devi must speak to us! At least a few words!' sparking off earsplitting shouts from the vast crowds. At the insistence of the leaders on the stage, Vasundhara got up, folded her hands in greeting and spoke a few sentences.

'Brothers and sisters! I am grateful to be honoured by you. I see it as your respect for service to the nation. I haven't done anything remarkable. To feed the hungry guest is an ancient tradition with us. I did nothing beyond my duty in feeding the two hungry volunteers who came to my doorstep. If such an opportunity had come your way, each one of you would have done the same. Vande mataram! Mahatma Gandhi ki jai!'

When the crowds dispersed after the meeting, it was inevitable that Vasundhara Devi should be the sole topic of discussion.

'Did you see how she lashed out! Didn't she say that if the opportunity had come our way each one of us would have done the same thing? Surely it would have stung those who banged their doors shut in sheer terror.'

Another cut in, 'Why talk of others? What about you and me?'

'Listen to me. It is time we took to wearing bangles and stayed at home,' said another enthusiast.

'Look, no one who wears pants in this town has the grit of this lady in a sari,' someone else observed with detached conviction.

'And how well she wears that sari! Think of the idiots at home winding eighteen yards around themselves!' said another, still in a state of ecstasy.

## 3

As soon as he went home Srikanthan described the meeting to his mother and sisters (two of them were always visiting).

34

They were astounded to hear that a woman had made a public speech.

'To which caste does she belong?' his mother asked.

'Hundred per cent brahmin, Amma! And smartha at that.'

'I wonder if she is vadama or ashtasahasram. Only from ashtasahasram can we expect this kind of boldness.'

'How smart of you! Is caste the most important thing? And you call yourselves women!' Srikanthan was bitter.

After a pause one of the sisters asked, 'How old is she?'

Srikanthan longed to talk to someone about Vasundhara Devi. And so he replied, 'About twenty-five.'

'Does she have a husband?' the second sister asked him.

'How does it concern you?'

'Why not? Why should we not be concerned? Is it right for a brahmin woman to remain unmarried beyond a certain age?'

One of the sisters whispered something to the mother at which she broke out in dismay. 'Siva, Siva! Did you see if there was a taali round her neck?' She shook her head and added, 'If I see her, I will certainly ask her about it. Who is she that I should be afraid of her?'

'Go to hell!' Srikanthan got up and walked away.

From then on, Srikanthan began to attend Congress meetings regularly. He made friends with some Congressmen. Soon he began to visit the party office as well. The town's

Congressmen were delighted that a wealthy young man, son of a retired sub-judge, should show such a keen interest in the party. Two months later, when the Congress committees were reconstituted, Srikanthan was appointed secretary of the district committee.

The next day he called on Vasundhara Devi at her home. They had become acquainted at meetings and public functions. 'I have accepted the post of secretary but you must help me discharge my duties,' he said to her. 'You must know I joined the Congress only because of you.'

Vasundhara was overwhelmed with joy. She had not expected such an event in her sad life.

'I am ready to help you. Nothing can make me happier. If I hesitate, it is only because the municipal chairman may have some reservations.'

'I will go and meet the chairman. Let him object if he likes. What is so great about this job of yours? Isn't the whole town with you in this? Shall we let you suffer?'

The municipal chairman raised no objections. That was the year of the Gandhi-Irwin treaty, and many persons had turned Congress supporters. Even government officials wished to please Congressmen.

In 1931 the Congress party established work centres all over Tamil Nadu. In this process of consolidation no other committee worked as zealously as the district committee of which Srikanthan was the secretary. At every opportune and inopportune moment Srikanthan kept saying that the entire credit for this achievement belonged to Vasundhara Devi.

Once when the two happened to be alone, Srikanthan said, 'We know each other so well, but I know nothing about your past. I have told you everything about my life. But you have not spoken a single word about yours. If you have no objections, I should be very eager to know more.'

'Ask me what you want to know and I will tell you.'

'Were you ever married?'

'Yes, I was. Would you like to see the proof?' Vasundhara turned and pushed the cloth a little away from her back. Two long black scars marked her fair skin.

Srikanthan closed his eyes. He recognized them as marks of branding.

'I was branded by my mother-in-law. My first offence was that I had cast a spell on her son. The second, that I did not keep quiet under torture. I wrote to my father.'

'I am amazed you can remain so cheerful after having undergone such a terrible experience.'

'At first music gave me some solace. Since my coming here, I have two reasons to be happy. I serve the nation. And . . . you know the other reasons.'

A lump in his throat reduced Srikanthan's response to a low mumble.

After a pause he said, 'When I listen to stories like this I feel that the nation's freedom is not such a vital issue. What is more important is to fight for social reform.'

'They are not mutually exclusive,' Vasundhara told him. 'We can serve the nation and society at the same time.'

One day Ramakrishna Iyer made Vasundhara sit by him and asked her, 'My dear, old as I am, I still get to hear all sorts of rumours about you and Srikanthan. Is there any truth in them?'

'What rumours, Appa?'

'They say you two are going to get married.'

'Do you disapprove? If that is so I shall not even dream of . . .'

'My child, I want you to be happy,' sighed Ramakrishna Iyer. 'Day and night I pray for you.'

At that time there was a change in the political scene. Mahatma Gandhi returned from the Second Round Table Conference in London. Viceroy Willingdon's turning down of Mahatma Gandhi's request for a meeting and the resumption of the satyagraha movement become events of historic significance.

'What is Srikanthan going to do?' was the question on everybody's lips. Only Srikanthan and Vasundhara had no doubts in the matter.

'Tomorrow six of us are starting the protest march from

38

the Congress office. But it looks as if we may not be able to reach the shopping area. Official orders are to make free use of lathis.'

'I shall come with you,' Vasundhara's voice quivered.

'Certainly not. If both of us are despatched on day one, the movement will come to an end. You must stay outside for at least two months more.'

After some argument Vasundhara agreed that Srikanthan was right, and promised to follow his advice.

'I don't know how I shall get through tomorrow. Every lash on your body will fall on my heart.'

In 1932 thousands of Indians were inspired by some divine power to become heroes of matchless valour. They went into the struggle in batches, expecting lathi charges, serious injury and hospitalization, followed by years of imprisonment. Srikanthan and his friends were among them. As the stick fell upon his rounded, muscular limbs which had never known pain or suffering, his voice continued to cry louder than ever, 'Vande Mataram!'

The police stopped the assault only when everyone fell senseless to the ground, and hauled them off to the prisonhouse. The next day they were all sentenced to six months' imprisonment.

On those two days Srikanthan's house was in an uproar. There was no end to the anxiety of his sisters. 'Ayyo, will father's pension be stopped?' The mother wailed in agony, 'Didn't I say long ago that he should have been shackled in marriage? Did anyone listen to me?'

How can you describe the retired sub-judge's state of mind? He had believed that the Congress would come to power and his son would find a job in that line of work. That was the reason he had not opposed Srikanthan's becoming the secretary of the Congress committee. But it had turned out to be a disaster.

4

Srikanthan's courage and spirit of sacrifice spurred the whole town to wonder. But few were ready to follow him. It was as if they had decided that if at all they wanted to go to prison, there were other, more likely routes like larceny or forgery. No, satyagraha was not one of them.

Vasundhara could not bear this apathy. For a week she struggled to get things moving. When she realized they were of no avail, she launched into public protest with two women volunteers. She was arrested and taken away. The others were sentenced to three months and Vasundhara to nine. It broke her heart to leave her old, infirm father alone and without support. But at that time there were many frenzied souls in the nation who dared as much.

No one was as cheerful as Vasundhara in the women's prison at Vellore.

Srikanthan was often in her thoughts. Her many speculations about the future ended with him. Finally she vowed to herself that since Providence had brought them together, they would face all opposition from society and spend their lives together in serving the nation.

Six months passed. Her longings grew fevered. Srikanthan would soon be free, he would come and visit her. Every day she waited for his letter.

A whole month went by in such anticipation. She wondered if he had plunged into action again and returned to prison. Couldn't he have stayed out at least until she was released?

Vasundhara became restive. 'Send me all the important news in town,' she wrote to her father. Some of the lines in his reply were struck out by the prison censors. There she thought she twice detected Srikanthan's name. Her tension mounted.

Her father also informed Vasundhara that a teaching post was offered to her at the sevashram where she had studied. After her release she could go to Madras and accept it.

The head of the sevashram was a rare human being. She had a special affection for Vasundhara. She made this offer

41

knowing that the municipal school may have no place for Vasundhara after a prison sentence.

Vasundhara's face registered a smile. Return to Madras? Join the sevashram? How could others know that her life was now linked to Srikanthan's?

## 5

Nine months rolled by. Vasundhara was free. But she did not experience even a fraction of the thrill she had expected at her release.

A few Congress sympathizers in Vellore came to take her to the railway station and put her on the train.

She did not sleep a wink that night. Every time the train stopped she felt an irresistible urge to make enquiries about Srikanthan's whereabouts from the people going to and fro on the platform.

Vasundhara disembarked as a free woman at the same station where nine months ago she had boarded the train a prisoner. But she felt none of the old exhilaration.

She looked around. The person she expected was not to be seen but the two women who had been arrested with her were there to receive her. They embraced her warmly, escorted her out of the station and to her home in a hired vehicle.

After routine exchanges about prison life Vasundhara asked them, 'Who is the Congress secretary here?'

'There is neither Congress nor secretary.'

'Why? What about Srikanthan?'

'Srikanthan! Why, haven't you heard the news?'

'No. Has he gone back to prison?' Vasundhara's heart beat fast.

'Why should he go back to prison? He's not that crazy.'

Vasundhara felt a little consoled. People were always ready to criticize others. Why should he rush back to gaol?

'Is he in town?' she asked.

'How can he be in town? He is getting married today in Pondicherry. You poor thing, how could you know?'

After a long silence Vasundhara asked in a low voice, 'Why in Pondicherry?'

'The bride is thirteen years old. They are holding the ceremony there to escape the Sarda Act.'

Her friends took leave of her at the door. Ramakrishna Iyer heard the vehicle arrive, and stopped playing the fiddle.

'My child!'

'Appa!' Vasundhara cried as she came running in to hug him. Father and daughter sobbed their hearts out.

Half an hour later when their weeping abated, Vasundhara said, 'Appa, please write to the sevashram. We can leave for Madras tomorrow.'

# THE GOVERNOR'S VISIT

'Governor Vijayam'
*Navashakti* (1925)

# 1

*S*riman Sivagurunathan Chettiar relaxed in his easy chair after lunch as usual, and picked up the newspaper. As he scanned the headlines he was startled by the announcement, 'Poikai Dam—Governor to lay foundation stone.'

Chettiar had goose bumps all over. His heart began to race. Controlling himself with an effort, he read on. The report gave details of the governor's arrival at the railway station on the 20th at 7 a.m. He was to take a car to the site of the dam.

Chettiar at once summoned his clerk Jayarama Iyer and asked him, 'Have you heard the news?'

'No sir, anything special?'

'How would you know anything? Don't I tell you again and again to read the papers? Why do we spend Rs 250 every year on the subscription? What would have happened if I hadn't followed the news carefully?'

'Sir, please give me the news.'

'The governor is paying a visit to our town on the 20th.'

The clerk's opened his mouth in wonder. He was too astonished to do anything except break into incoherent exclamations.

'All right, what do we do next?'

'We must get everything organized.'

47

'I must be at the railway station on the 20th morning. Make sure our car is shining and spotless.'

'Didn't I insist you should buy a motor car? Wasn't it an excellent suggestion?'

'My dear man, it is that foresight which makes you so valuable to me . . . Well, shouldn't we get our house decorated for the occasion?'

'Why, is the governor going past our home?'

'I'm not sure. He may go straight to the site from the station. I must persuade the Collector durai to take him through our street.'

'It doesn't matter. In any case, the fact that our house is being decorated will be reported in the papers.'

'True enough. But will the news of the governor's arrival escape the eyes of Kurmavataram Iyengar? Does he not read the papers as keenly as I do?'

'Don't worry. Even if he gets to know, there is nothing much he can do about it. First of all, he has no motor car, only an old fashioned coach. Don't you remember how the whole durbar burst into laughter when Iyengar accepted the Rao Bahadur title from the Collector, dressed like a clown and bowing as if he would never stop? The same thing will happen again.'

Chettiar chuckled as he recalled that old scene. 'Still, he must not know our plans. Keep everything ready and put up

48

the festoons on the night of the 19th after 10 p.m. Let Iyengar get up and blink in the morning.'

Chettiar and Iyer held long discussions about the necessary preparations. Finally they were struck by a bright idea. Chettiar sent a message to the president of the town council saying that at their next meeting, he would propose the presentation of a citation to the governor. After that the clerk went about his usual business.

Sivagurunathan Chettiar was a prosperous businessman. He owned the only three-storeyed mansion in his little town. He had started life as a poor clerk in a hardware store. But soon the goddess Lakshmi cast him a little glance from the corner of her eye, and Chettiar opened his own shop and business. His wealth increased day by day. His large pre-war stock of iron doubled and tripled in value during the World War. Chettiar became a millionaire overnight.

He began to crave social recognition. His next door neighbour, the advocate Kurmavataram Iyengar, became his role model in the social graces and sartorial style. Chettiar engaged a tutor to teach him English. He adopted all the ostentations of high living. He threw frequent parties for government officers. He squandered an enormous sum to become town councillor. Presently his entire ambition was focussed on obtaining the Rao Bahadur title.

A sneaking fear plagued him. What if Iyengar became

Dewan Bahadur before that? He intended to overtake Iyengar by hook or by crook in securing the governor's favour. That is the reason the Iyengar figured repeatedly in his conversations with his clerk.

The next day Chettiar attended the council meeting with a beaming face. His well-prepared proposal to present a citation to the governor was tucked into his shirt pocket.

His speech was divided into three parts. Part one described the benefits of British rule in India. Part two had details of the governor's ancestry, family history, character traits and individual merits. The third part listed all the contributions of the governor, real and imaginary, to the welfare of the state.

At the end of his peroration, Chettiar drew the kind attention of the esteemed governor to the single regrettable act of omission in his regime. Loyal subjects of the crown were not given sufficient recognition or reward. He humbly prayed that the governor show discrimination in the conferment of titles on deserving persons.

The clerk sent copies of the proposal to all reporters with the assurance that Chettiar would bear the cost of telegraphing the whole speech to their respective headquarters. The reporters were also invited to Chettiar's home the day after the governor's visit.

But alas! The moment he took his seat in the council

Chettiar's joy turned to grief and anger. He came to know that Rao Bahadur Iyengar had sent his claim to make a similar proposal before Chettiar had. He would therefore get precedence in the matter. But Chettiar was not a man to be stumped by reversals. Life had taught him that determined effort achieved results. He successfully manoeuvred the right to second Iyengar's proposal. From that it was but an easy step to read the entire speech in the guise of seconding the proposal. Poor man, how could he know Iyengar had made arrangements to prevent his speech from reaching the newsrooms?

As Chettiar cursed God and man, his clerk brought him information which consoled him a little.

'The Governor arrives at the station at 7 a.m. He has to travel fifty miles to be at the River Poikai by 9 a.m. to lay the dam's foundation stone. He has no time to receive the citation at the town council or at the railway station. This message came just now from the governor's personal secretary . . . Good thing you did not propose the citation. You have been spared a loss of face.'

Chettiar was very glad. 'Ah, Kurmavataram Iyengar got what he deserved. Didn't he try to steal a march over me?'

'All the same, shouldn't you be at the station on the 20th morning?'

'Of course. All our other plans stand as before.'

51

## 2

At last, the appointed day arrived. Chettiar was up at dawn. After his bath and breakfast, he stood before the mirror for a good half-hour making his toilette. His dear wife was beside him, smoothening the folds of his garments and polishing his jewels. As soon as he was ready, he sent the clerk to fetch the car from the garage. Chettiar's wife took a look at the street outside to check if the signs favoured her husband's trip. When the omens and the time were auspicious, Chettiar stepped out of the house and entered his car. A big flapping Union Jack graced the car's bonnet.

Chettiar felt a pang when he saw his neighbour's house. Iyengar too had played a waiting game through the previous day and had put up flags and festoons in the dark. The car began to move and there was little time for more speculation.

It took five minutes to reach the station. Chettiar saw that Iyengar was there before him, ready for action. Their fierce competitiveness remained strictly hidden. To the world they were the best of friends.

'What brings you here so early?' Chettiar enquired.

'A small errand. I heard you were leaving for Madras. Is that why you are here?' Iyengar asked mischievously.

'Never mind. But tell me, your house has been festooned with decorations overnight. Any special occasion?'

'I saw festoons in your house too. Is it true that you are celebrating your sixtieth birthday?' Iyengar's query had a sarcastic ring to it.

Chettiar wished to give him a severe set down but suddenly the station was filled with people. There were members of the town council, taluk and zillah board; graduates and those struggling to become graduates; advocates, officers, members of the security force; volunteers who had come to stage a political protest and watch the fun at the same time; representatives of the secret police who shadowed the volunteers. All of them stood cheek by jowl, their eyes straining to remain unblinkingly fixed on the railway track.

Finally the governor's special train arrived. Police officers strode up and down to establish the peace. The honourable governor disembarked. A path was cleared for him. All those who had come with manifold dreams stood breathless in adoration—pounding hearts and earnest eyes. They trembled lest the honourable governor leave without a single glance at them. Later it was learnt that an ardent soul among the multitude had fainted in rapture, but so great was his loyalty to the crown that, determined to cause no confusion, he stood upright, even in such an extreme condition, clutching the pillar which hid him.

Meanwhile, the governor took off his hat as a mark of civility and held it in his hand. His sweeping glance surveyed the crowd from one end to the other. Everyone present knew it was the moment of fulfilment of a lifetime ambition. They were petrified by the thought that the governor might miss their salute in the precise moment his eye rested on them. They continued to salute him until he left the station. For a full five minutes their hands kept touching their foreheads and dropping down, like forest branches swaying incessantly in the west wind.

Having brought everyone under his royal glance, the governor swiftly walked out and got into the waiting car. And those who had come to be exalted by the gracious sight returned to their respective homes.

Sriman Sivagurunathan Chettiar reached home safe and sound. At once he was surrounded by an excited group of wife, children, clerk and staff. Chettiar was a kind man. He did not wish to disappoint so many eager souls.

'We must call the priest to arrange a special thanksgiving to the temple deity. Things went off very well today.'

'Did the governor speak to you? What did you say to him? What actually happened?' everyone wanted to know.

'As soon as he got off the train, the governor spoke to one or two officials like the zillah collector and came straight to me,' Chettiar told them. 'Do you think I felt the slightest fear? Not at all! He shook my hand and said, "Chettiar, I have heard a lot about you. How do you do? Are your friends

54

and relatives doing well?" You know me. Once I start talking I cannot stop. I said, "Your Excellency, under your rule we have no complaints. But I am forced to express my discontent over the fact that your government shows no discrimination in awarding titles."

'Ayyayyo! That was severe! Didn't the governor get angry?' the clerk asked with concern.

The words gushed forth from Chettiar's lips. 'Angry? What do you mean? As soon as I said this, the governor shook my hand again and said, "Chettiar, thank you very much for bringing this to my attention. I will take steps to rectify the matter." The crowd broke into applause. But you should have seen our Rao Bahadur Iyengar. He was dumbstruck. He was standing in an obsure corner. No one took the slightest notice of him.'

At that very instant, if anyone had eavesdropped in the women's quarters at Rao Bahadur Kurmavataram Iyengar's house, he would have heard Iyengar say to his beloved spouse, 'But the governor did not waste a single glance on Sivagurunathan Chettiar. Poor thing! He stood in an obscure corner and slunk away quite unnoticed.'

# RURAL FANTASY

'Kanaiyazhiyin Kanavu'
*Ananda Vikatan* (1934)

# 1. Sakuntalai's Choice

*I*t was only a dream. But what a delightful dream!

Trijata narrated her dream to Sita in Asokavana. Sita listened with great joy. Trijata ended her account, '. . . I saw the lotus-eyed goddess entering Vibhishana's abode with a lamp of a thousand flames in her hand. I awoke at that crucial moment . . .' Thereupon Sita beseeched her to sleep again and tell her the rest of the dream.

('What's this? A research paper, on the Ramayana?')

No, no. I only gave an example. When Raghuraman awoke from his dream, he found himself in more or less the same frame of mind. Like Sita, he too yearned to return to sleep and see the rest of his dream.

('Raghuraman? Who's he?')

Please forgive me. Not the hero of the Ramayana. This is K.P. Raghuraman, BA, of Kanaiyazhi.

('Kanaiyazhi? What's that?')

Good Lord! Not Rama's signet ring Kanaiyazhi which was handed over to Sita by Hanuman. This is the name of the village where my story took place. How the village got its name is another story. It can be told later. Now I will tell you about Raghuraman's wonderful dream.

Sakuntalai . . . This is not her real name. I changed it because I feared readers would not tolerate yet another name

59

from the Ramayana. Well, Sakuntalai leaned back and dangled her legs from her merry perch on a low branch of the riverside peepul tree. She held a flower garland in her right hand. K.P. Raghuraman and the other young men of the village—who possessed all the qualifications of the Romantic Hero—were practising sit-ups under the tree.

One after another they began to drop out of the exercise. One, two, three, four . . . All gone except for Raghuraman and Vaidyanathan. Finally Vaidyanathan collapsed in defeat.

'Raghuraman is the winner. I choose to garland him,' said Sakuntalai in a voice sweeter than birdsong and harpstring. She started climbing down. Raghuraman leapt up to help her. It was at this enchanting, delectable and breathless juncture that he awoke. He took stock of himself. He had left his bed to stand in the verandah, one hand on the pillar and another on the low rafter. His heart ached to sleep again and recapture that vision. But no, he couldn't sleep a wink. His mind was filled with impossible thoughts.

He realized that the dream was the result of his evening conversation with the young men of the village.

'Why can't we hold a swayamvaram now as they did in the past? What if he who performs the bravest deed among us could marry Sakuntalai?' asked Kalyanasundaram.

'So you imagine you'll win?' asked Ramamurti. Everyone laughed when Vaidyanathan declared, 'I only know that if we hold a competition in sit-ups, Raghuraman will win hands down.'

There was some truth in Vaidyanathan's statement. Raghuraman had practised sit-ups since childhood. He could do three to four hundred at a time.

The young men argued about the feats in which each could beat the others. Raghuraman was a little ashamed to think that he should have dreamt about the teasing he had received.

Never mind. The others would not come to know. As far as Raghuraman was concerned, he was content to dream the same dream without ever awakening, through an entire lifetime.

There were many in Kanaiyazhi who had similar dreams that night. Vaidyanathan saw himself seated in a row with Ramamurti, Raghuraman *et al*, plaintain leaves laid before them. A large dish filled with idlis, and jars full of oil and chilli powder stood waiting.

Sakuntalai began to serve them the idlis, keeping scores on a black board of the numbers they consumed. Others stopped with eight, ten, fifteen, eighteen . . . However, Vaidyanathan went relentlessly on. He felt that with such a lovely, flower-like hand circled by a single ivory bangle to serve him, it was child's play to swallow all the idlis in the dish. He could eat idlis endlessly, forever . . .

When he came to the forty-eighth idli, Sakuntalai stepped forward with a garland and opened her coralline lips to announce, 'Vaidyanathan is the winner. I shall garland him.' At that instant, perhaps thanks to his excessive delight, the forty-eighth idli stuck in his throat. Vaidyanathan gabbled and choked as he sat up in bed. He discovered that the muffler wrapped around his head to ward off chills, had tightened into a knot. He loosened its hold.

## 2. Calcutta Ranganatham

Kanaiyazhi is a fertile village on the banks of the river Arunai. The inhabitants boasted a generations-old heritage of shrewdness. They did not put their trust in Dhanya Lakshmi—Goddess of Plentiful Harvests—alone. They offered worship to their favoured patron Dhana Lakshmi—Goddess of Wealth. They wooed her with the moneylenders' mantra of 'interest' and 'compound interest'. Enslaved by this magic formula, Dhana Lakshmi served them faithfully.

In such a village it was not surprising that members of the younger generation should have had an 'English' education. Those above twenty years of age were either graduates, post-graduates, or had travelled part way through the course. And so wealthy that they did not bother to hunt for jobs. Let the jobs come hunting for them!

Calcutta Ranganatham was a member of the older

generation who lived in the village at that time. Though born in Kanaiyazhi he was the odd man out who had nothing to do with the money lending business. He had recently retired with a pension as the accountant-general in Calcutta. His long-term residence in that city was the reason why he was identified as Calcutta Ranganatham. Two years ago when his wife and son had died, he had left his daughter Sakuntalai in Tagore's Santiniketan and returned to Kanaiyazhi. He engaged a cook and set up a home to live all by himself. His books, which filled five or six cupboards, were his sole companions.

The young men in the village did visit him now and then for chats. That is, they chatted and he listened. At times the visitors wondered if he really heard them or only pretended to do so. Many subjects were discussed. When the question of C.K. Nayudu's home town came up one of them insisted he was from Tamil Nadu while another was equally sure he was a Bangalore man. When they appealed to him Ranganatham gave a start and said 'Sarojini Naidu? A Bengali lady. No doubt about it.'

One day the young men were greatly surprised to see such a dreamy soul breaking into excited and energetic talk. He made minute enquiries about the names, number and timings of trains which came into the Kanaiyazhi station. Next he asked them about roads around the village suitable

63

for car travel. He also wanted to know if any of the young men were married. He could not hide his amusement when he learnt that Sridharan was engaged to a girl of fourteen. 'Do such dolls' weddings take place even in these days?' he said in surprise. And he expressed his own conviction that when a woman became an adult, she should be free to choose her own partner in life.

Ranganatham asked many more questions. Did the village have any educated women? Were there associations for women to get together? Soon the youngsters came to know the reason for his sudden interest in Kanaiyazhi's social life. His daughter Sakuntalai, who had completed her studies in Santiniketan, was to arrive by the next morning's train. She would be staying in Kanaiyazhi for three months.

The young men of Kanaiyazhi went to bed that night with a feeling that they were in for the <u>most unusual experience</u> of their lives.

## 3. The New Woman

What could have brought so many people to the railway station in the morning? Raghuraman chatted animatedly with the clerk at the ticket counter. But his eyes strayed frequently towards the hands of the clock.

Vaidyanathan was holding an animated conversation with porter Chinnappan. Sridharan was strolling on the platform

64

as if on the Madras beach. Seated on the weighing machine, Kalyanasundaram scanned the advertisement pages of the previous day's newspaper with single-minded devotion.

The train arrived. Ranganatham hastened towards the ladies' compartment. Raghuraman had never seen him walk so fast. The next moment he saw the full moon emerge from the ladies' coach. Dear me! Was that really a woman's face? What's this? A row of pearls on the luminous moon? What a dazzling smile; 'Appa, I'm here!' Were the words dipped in honey? Or mixed with nectar? Raghuraman's feet moved automatically towards the pair.

Before Sakuntalai got down with her luggage, the young men of Kanaiyazhi—each endowed with all the qualifications for top billing as hero—clustered around them. Porter Chinnappan witnessed a miracle, for the first and only time in his career. The young masters who would normally enlist him to carry even a briefcase, now grabbed the suitcase, bedroll and other pieces of luggage and carried them away.

Ranganatham and Sakuntalai got into the vehicle after the luggage was loaded. 'Righto! We'll come in the evening to talk about other things,' said Vaidyanathan.

'Yes, come in the evening,' Ranganatham replied. On the way home he scratched his bald pate when Sakuntalai asked him, 'What other things?'

On that day, evening arrived at two o'clock in the

afternoon and well before 3 p.m., seven or eight young men, including Raghuraman and Vaidyanathan, gathered in Ranganatham's house. Ranganatham welcomed them with unusual warmth. He even ordered the cook to serve them coffee, something he had never done before.

Sakuntalai came with the coffee. 'This is my daughter. I spoke to you about her yesterday,' Ranganatham told them.

'We guessed as much this morning,' Kalyanasundaram said.

'You guessed right but let me introduce her properly now.'

Sakuntalai intervened, 'But you haven't introduced them to me.'

'True. That's exactly what I'm about to do. This is Vaidyanathan.' Loud merriment greeted his words because Ranganatham had pointed to Kalyanasundaram.

'My name is Kalyanasundaram. That is Vaidyanathan,' said Kalyanasundaram.

The person thus pointed out added, 'Vaidyanathan MA' in mock deprecation. He intended to seize the chance to display his credentials.

'Appa is hopeless with names—of people and places. Appa, do you at least remember my name?'

This sally triggered explosive laughs. But Raghuraman did not join in. For the last half-hour he had been lost in a reverie. He longed to speak to Sakuntalai but what could he say?

66

At long last he mustered enough courage to ask, 'What's the news from Calcutta?'

'In Calcutta? So much is happening there!' Sakuntalai responded. At that time the freedom movement was spreading throughout over the nation. Calcutta was a hotbed of nationalist activity. Sakuntalai described incidents connected to the movement. Everyone hung upon her words, wide-eyed and open-mouthed.

Before she went to bed, Sakuntalai said to Ranganatham, 'Appa, the village boys seem to be totally crazy.'

'Did you say crazy?'

'Yes.'

'That's good.'

'What's good about it?' Sakuntalai smiled.

'I had thought them stupid. But you say they are merely crazy.'

With a bigger laugh Sakuntalai asked him, 'What do you mean, Appa? Is a crackpot better than a fool?'

'Certainly. You can't do anything with fools. But you can get some work out of crackpots.'

'I do plan to get some work out of them. Let's see.'

## 4. The Furore

There was a girl's school in Kanaiyazhi. Kanakasabhai was the instructor. A man of the old world. Ayyo, swami! Never in his life had he been thrown into such a frightful muddle.

'Saar, Saar! Somebody is coming, saar!' a girl shouted. It was the signal for all the girls to rush to the window. The vadiyar took a look. At once the school, the bench, chair, table and inkstand began to spin around him. Desperately did he grab the blackboard's duster cloth and wind it round his head in a turban. He snatched the turban cloth from the table and tossed it over his shoulder. He picked up his angavastram on the back of the chair and blinked in utter dismay.

By then he could hear the visitors' footsteps. So he stuffed the cloth into the table drawer and hissed menacingly at the girls, 'Shut up and sit down! To your places!'

The next moment Srimati Sakuntala Devi and her father entered the classroom.

'Vadiyar! This is my daughter. She has come from Calcutta. I brought her here because she wanted to see the school,' said Ranganatham. It took a while for the vadiyar to make sense of his words. He had been dreadfully rattled because he had mistaken Sakuntalai for one of those school inspectors who made sudden descents upon the unwary. Didn't they make inspectresses out of young chits and send them to frighten old men out of their wits?

Smiling at his attempts to spruce up, Sakuntalai said, 'I hope you don't mind.'

68

'Mind what?'

'I want to come every day and teach these children songs. May I?'

Kanakasabhai vadiyar recovered his powers of speech. 'I have been waiting for someone to make such an offer. So many people in the village but not a single one to pay some attention to the school. They send their children here because the kids are a nuisance at home. Even that they don't do regularly. They only come to grumble about a child being weak in maths or not being able to sing . . .' The vadiyar aired his own grievances.

Sakuntalai spent a little time making friends with the girls, learning their names and classes. Then she taught them two lines of a Hindi song about the Indian flag.

'Jhanda ooncha rahe hamara . . .'

She left promising to come again.

A strange sight met their eyes as father and daughter walked home. Surprisingly, all the men and women in the village had important work which had brought them out of their houses. The men and the older women were seen sitting on the pyols. Young girls peeped from behind doors and from windows opened to a crack. The news of Sakuntalai's visit to the village school had drawn all of them out to wait for a glimpse of the girl from Calcutta.

Kanaiyazhi was in a state of ferment.

69

## 5. Revolution

Since Sakuntalai's arrival, the young men of Kanaiyazhi felt the frequent need for consultations with Calcutta Ranganatham. He was now the only person who could solve their problems or clear their doubts in any matter.

At one of those convivial gatherings Sakuntalai declared, 'I hate this place. I don't know why I came here.' Ranganatham turned a startled face towards her.

'Why do you say that? What is it you dislike here? Isn't Kanaiyazhi famous as the loveliest village in this district?' asked Kalyanasundaram.

'The village is certainly beautiful. But the people are awful. The streets are always dirty. A garbage dump near the school, a cattle shed beside the temple. It is impossible to set foot on the street where the field hands live. The trash and the stench are unbearable. I tried to take that route yesterday but had to turn back in a hurry,' Sakuntalai said.

'What to do my dear? That's our way of life,' her father told her. 'Only Englishmen keep their streets and surroundings clean. Don't know when we'll imbibe some civic sense from them.'

'If these friends make up their minds things can change in no time. You should come and see the villages near Santiniketan. Do you know how clean they are? If educated people show the way initially, others will automatically learn

70

to keep their village clean,' Sakuntalai suggested.

We do not know how the miracle took place. But within two or three days, no one knew where all the garbage disappeared. The young men of the village developed a keen interest in matters of hygiene. They talked hygiene all the time, in and out of their homes. Their efforts began to bear fruit even in the streets where people of the lower castes lived. If only hens and pigs could talk, they would have filed vociferous complaints against these young men of Kanaiyazhi who starved them. Even the field labourers began to grumble, 'If the young masters continue this cleaning rampage for three months, there will be no manure left for the crops.' In this manner, every aspect of Kanaiyazhi's social life underwent radical reform.

## 6. Downpour

On another occasion Sakuntalai spoke in bitter dejection. She hated life. 'Why do we live in this world? Women in particular should not prolong their days on earth. In the past it seems it was the custom to throw the girl-child into the Ganga. Appa, why didn't you do that to me?'

Ranganatham registered astonishment. The hearts of Raghuraman, Vaidyanathan, Kalyanasundaram *et al* who were present, writhed in agony. Each one of them vowed he would give his own life to save Sakuntalai.

71

'Why do you say that my dear?' Ranganathan asked her gently.

'As your daughter I lead a pleasant life. What if I had been born Sornammal?'

'Who is Sornammal?' Sridharan enquired. Everyone felt indescribable compassion for her.

'Sornammal is our housemaid,' Sakuntalai replied. The men lost much of their interest.

'What about her?'

Sakuntalai described her plight, 'Sornammal is my age. She is seven months pregnant. This morning she began to cry when I told her not to come to work any more, I would engage a new maid. She said her husband would kill her if she lost this job. She showed me the scars of all the battering she has received. Even last evening her husband came home roaring drunk and hollered, 'Where is our little son? Bring him to me this instant . . .'

Raghuraman and his friends laughed.

'I was amused too when I first heard it. But when I saw the bruises on Sornam, I felt miserable. It seems her husband Ponnan bawled further, 'You bitch, you have murdered my beloved son,' and beat her black and blue. She is afraid he will actually murder her if she stopped going to work.'

Tears stood in Sakuntalai's eyes. 'Who knows how many women suffer like this? Isn't there some way of getting rid of

72

this evil? I hear that even respectable men in this village lease their palm trees for brewing country liquor. Atrocious!'

From that day Kanaiyazhi village began to witness scenes of evening farce.

You saw Raghuraman and Kalyanasundaram flanking the local drunk who howled out dialogues from street theatre, 'Wise Minister Satyakirti! How dare you abduct my beloved Surpanakha and refuse to return her to me? If you do not return her forthwith I shall order Indrajit to slice your head off!'

'Ponnan, look here,' said Raghuraman. 'Liquor destroys the family. It is a great evil. Give it up.'

## 7. Earthquake

The female community in Kanaiyazhi was in a state of mental turmoil. Hidebound beliefs and diehard customs disappeared into the yawning cracks of that upheaval.

When Chandrasekharan entered his bedroom one night he saw an incredible sight. His helpmeet Srimati Saradambal was holding Harihara Iyer's first English reader in her hand and enunciating conscientiously, 'P-I-G, pig.'

'My goodness! What is this sudden passion for English?' he teased.

'You only know how to make fun of me. Do you ever stop to think that I too should have some education like other people?' said Sarada. Her large black eyes were on the brink of tears. But poor Chandrasekharan was too much of a dumb male to notice it. He told her, 'Shall I tell you why? You want to be like Sakuntalai!'

A sob broke out. 'Don't I know it, you are constantly thinking of her.' And then the floods came. Chandrasekharan was lost in its currents and struggled through a good part of the night to reach the shores.

When the gossip council of the womenfolk of Kanaiyazhi met the next day, the subject of debate was the Calcutta girl. This story is already overloaded with names. Anyway, the names are not important here. So I shall merely summarize the debate.

'I have seen some strange things in my time. Now we have this Calcutta girl phenomenon! Who knows what stranger things are in store for me before the end?'

'If that wretch Parvati had not died, this girl would have been brought up differently.'

'It seems Parvati had a dreadful time with her husband. He dragged her willy-nilly into all his freakish starts. Her sufferings made her drown herself in the Ganga.'

'She could have pushed this girl into the river before she drowned herself. The problem would have been solved.'

'Why do you say such harsh things, aunt? What is wrong with Sakuntalai? She is like a princess. Does she have to be chained to the kitchen like us?' said a youthful voice.

'No kitchen for her. Let her stand in the open streets. She is old enough to have had four children but she wanders around like cattle do. And you ask me what's wrong with her?'

'What have those who have borne four children achieved that she has missed? Looked at Ammini in the corner house. Not yet seventeen, she has had her third child. Every morning she starts beating her children. If you ask me, I'll say it is Sakuntalai who is fortunate.'

'Yes, my dear, yes. Why don't start you strolling through the streets, slippers on your feet and umbrella in your hand?'

'Can you become another Sakuntalai by merely wearing slippers and carrying an umbrella? What about her education and intelligence?'

'What's so special about her, did she come leaping out of the skies? If I had been educated I too would have been her equal. She's nothing superior!'

'That's right, you too could have attended school, passed exams and romped everywhere with the end of your sari flying in the breeze. You want all the bachelors in town to flock around you and go traipsing with you?'

'Chee! How you tongue runs on! Age has not given you a sense of what's decent and proper. Is this the way to talk?'

Very soon opinion was sharply divided among the younger

and older members of the Kanaiyazhi gossip council. The youth faction began to feel sympathy and affinity for Sakuntalai. They defended her at every turn. This trend began when Janaki boldly invited Sakuntalai to her house for manjal-kumkumam. Sakuntalai quickly made friends with the other young women who had come there for the occasion. Soon the young women of Kanaiyazhi developed an unprecedented passion for books and studies. Once when Sakuntalai found Lalitha with a novel in her hand and asked to see it, Lalitha said, 'This is in Tamil. You won't understand it.'

Sakuntalai laughed. 'What do you mean? You think I don't know Tamil? It is my mother tongue.'

'No, but since you have spent so many years in the north I assumed you would not know Tamil.'

'Not at all. In fact, living in the north makes you love Tamil even more. The Bengalis read books mostly in their own language. They laugh at southerners for being so English-mad.'

'All said and done, there's nothing like knowing English.'

'I don't agree. English is the white man's language. Tamil is our mother tongue. The best thing for us is to read and speak our own language.'

Sakuntalai attended the first birthday celebrations of Andalu's son. At the function the village women sang the songs they knew, mostly the Telugu kritis of Tyagaraja like 'Marukelara', 'Sujana jivana', 'Nagumomu', 'Dinamani vamsa' . . . 'Does no one know Tamil songs?' Sakuntalai asked.

'I only know nalangu songs, they are not very good,' Janaki answered.

'Not even Bharati's songs?' Lalitha heard Sakuntalai's persistent query and spoke out, 'Our Alamelu knows Bharati's songs. Alamelu! Sakuntalai wants to hear a Bharati song. Why don't you sing one?' After initially making a fuss, Alamelu let herself be persuaded into singing a song about Lala Lajpat Rai, the faithful supporter of the British Raj. Sakuntalai could barely restrain her giggles as she thought of the transformation of Lala Lajpat Rai, who had been exiled from the country for his seditious activities, into the loyal servant of the British crown! But she controlled herself. Alamelu was requested to sing again. This time she began with the patriotic cry of 'Vande Mataram' and ended with a description of the grand fair at Travancore.

After the function Sakuntalai told her friends that Alamelu's songs had not been authored by Bharati.

'Do you know Bharati's songs?' asked Janaki.

'No. But I have a book of his verses. If you come to my house we can set them to tune and learn to sing them. I will also teach you Hindustani and Bengali songs,' Sakuntalai offered.

77

'We would like to come. But the men haunt your house all the time!' Lalitha exclaimed.

'What does it matter? Why should they scare you off? They should be scared of you,' answered Sakuntalai.

Within ten-fifteen days every young woman in Kanaiyazhi began to believe that Sakuntalai was her best friend.

## 8. Hurricane

It was three months since Sakuntalai had come to Kanaiyazhi. The mental turbulence of the young men of Kanaiyazhi could be compared only to the hurricane-ravaged woods.

Why youngsters, even men of forty were swept off their feet. When his wife had died two years ago, Sriman Ramasubrahmanyam had resolved that the wedded state was not for him. He had refused all offers of remarriage. Now, for the sake of Sakuntalai, he was ready to reconsider his decision. He asked himself, is there anyone in this whole country fit to marry a girl like Sakuntalai with her attributes of education and intelligence? Well may youngsters smirk and show their teeth. But none of them can match her mature mind or make her a suitable husband. If Sakuntalai married a youngster she would ruin her life. I am the only man who can make her a proper partner in life.

If this was the condition of a man of forty, the state of twenty and twenty-five-year-olds could well be imagined. As the days passed the raging storm increased in velocity.

Sridharan managed to cancel his wedding. The reasons he gave were that he wished to wait for another year. He had plans of doing the BL course. With the law as his profession he could not afford to indulge in the illegal act of marrying a girl of twelve. When Sakuntalai congratulated him on his decision, he indicated to her that he did not object to marrying at once a girl who had reached the proper age.

Kuppuswami had been married for two years. But now he had developed a keen interest in divorce rights. He launched into perorations on the subject all the time. 'Our social contracts are extremely unjust. It is natural for man to err. Is there no way to rectify errors? We get married with the best of intentions. But when we realize it's a mistake, why can't both parties consult each other and right the wrong? I don't say this for the man's convenience. After all a man can marry as many times as he likes! Divorce is an essential advantage for women. Better to die once and for all than to be trapped in an unhappy relationship and suffer throughout one's life!'

The unmarried men of Kanaiyazhi had but one thought to occupy them day and night: how could they find Sakuntalai alone? How could they express their inmost dreams to her? It became more and more difficult to find an opportunity to do so.

79

As if the continual visits of the young men were not enough, Ranganatham's house and garden became the haunt of young women as well. The men slipped away as soon as they sighted the ladies. Sakuntalai teased them about it. 'What is this? What do you fear in the village girls that you don't fear in me?' she scoffed. When they were too bemused to reply she added, 'You are terribly unfair. Most of you are college-educated but you keep your women-folk in a state of blind ignorance. At least if you had been uneducated like your grandfathers, there would have been some justification to your making grandmothers of your wives.'

The thought of their future wives in the image of their grandmothers made the young men burst into uncontrollable guffaws. Raghuraman declared after a moment's thought, 'I am willing to give equal rights to my wife in everything.' But it didn't seem as if Sakuntalai caught his meaning.

In this matter Kalyanasundaram had a similar experience. When Sakuntalai expressed a wish to see the girls' school in the neighbouring village, Kalyanasundaram eagerly offered to escort her. He resolved to make use of this rare opportunity to pour out his flaming love for her. But it was not easy to find the words.

After prolonged hesitation, he stumbled into speech. 'Sakuntalai, don't you feel we are racing towards a place unknown?'

80

'Are we? I thought we were moving very slowly. Not even two-and-a-half miles per hour.'

After this he couldn't find anything to say for a while. But a pair of birds on a branch gave him an idea.

'I wish we could both turn into birds. Then, without a care in the world, we can soar blissfully across the skies forever.'

'But now that aircraft have been invented, man can fly as birds do. Ten years from now, airplanes will be commonplace. You and I and everybody else can fly effortlessly,' was Sakuntalai's response.

## 9. Peace

The news of a guest from Calcutta to Ranganatham's home flashed across Kanaiyazhi. He seemed to be a northerner. Ranganatham and his daughter had received him at the railway station. Sakuntalai held his hand as they walked on the station platform together—these were details which came through the wireless information service.

Fortunately Kanaiyazhi did not have to wait too long to know the truth. Ranganatham invited all his young acquaintances to tea that evening. When everyone arrived he introduced his new guest. 'This is Shyam babu, Sakuntalai's husband. I invited you today to introduce him.' The young man was a Bengali of about twenty-five.

And what of the reaction of the young men present on

the occasion? I don't know what the tenets of the code of love say in this matter. I know only what actually transpired.

The tornado which had raged in their souls for the last three months subsided at once. They were filled with a peace deep and complete. Their elation was a thing of the past now. On that day no one spilt coffee on his shirt.

They learnt several facts from Shyam babu. He was a professor in a Calcutta university. He had been sentenced to two year's imprisonment for his participation in the satyagraha movement. The scar on his forehead was the result of being wounded in a police crackdown. He was returning to Calcutta to take up his university job again.

'I am extremely grateful to all of you. I was worried about getting through these three months. Your friendship made the time pass happily and usefully,' Sankuntalai told them. 'We start in two or three days on a sightseeing trip through Tamil Nadu after which the return to Calcutta. I feel sorry to leave you all.'

On the fourth day after this meeting, they found a lock hanging on Calcutta Ranganatham's house.

As before, loads of trash began to litter the streets of Kanaiyazhi.

# THE TIGER KING

'Puliraja'
*Kalki* (1941)

# 1

$\mathcal{T}$he Maharaja of Pratibandapuram is the hero of this story. He may be identified as His Highness Jamedar-General, Khiledar-Major, Sata Vyaghra Samhari, Maharajadhiraja Visva Bhuvana Samrat, Sir Jilani Jung Jung Bahadur, M.A.D., A.C.T.C., C.R.C.K. But this name is often shortened to the Tiger King.

I have come forward to tell you why he came to be known as Tiger King. I have no intention of pretending to advance only end to in a strategic withdrawal. Even the threat of a Stuka bomber will not throw me off track. The Stuka, if it likes, can beat a hasty retreat from my story.

Right at the start, it is imperative to disclose a matter of vital importance about the Tiger King. Everyone who reads of him will experience the natural desire to meet a man of his indomitable courage face-to-face. But there is no chance of its fulfilment. As Bharata said to Rama about Dasaratha, the Tiger King has reached that final abode of all living creatures. In other words, the Tiger King is dead.

The manner of his death is a matter of extraordinary interest. It can be revealed only at the end of the tale. The most fantastic aspect of his demise was that as soon as he was born, astrologers had foretold that one day the Tiger King would actually have to die.

'The child will grow up to become the warrior of warriors, hero of heroes, champion of champions. But . . .' they bit their lips and swallowed hard. When compelled to continue, the astrologers came out with it. 'This is a secret which should not be revealed at all. And yet we are forced to speak out. The child born under this star will one day have to meet its death.'

At that very moment a great miracle took place. An astonishing phrase emerged from the lips of the ten-day-old Jilani Jung Jung Bahadur, 'O wise prophets!'

Everyone stood transfixed in stupefaction. They looked wildly at each other and blinked.

'O wise prophets! It was I who spoke.'

This time there were no grounds for doubt. It was the infant born just ten days ago which enunciated the words so clearly.

The chief astrologer took off his spectacles and gazed intently at the babe.

'All those who are born will one day have to die. We don't need your predictions to know that. There would be some sense in it if you could tell us the manner of that death,' the royal infant uttered these words in his little squeaky voice.

The chief astrologer placed his finger on his nose in wonder. A babe barely ten days old opens its lips in speech! Not only that, it also raises intelligent questions! Incredible! Rather like the bulletins issued by the war office, than facts.

The chief astrologer took his finger off his nose and fixed his eyes upon the little prince.

'The prince was born in the hour of the Bull. The Bull and the Tiger are enemies, therefore, death comes from the Tiger,' he explained.

You may think that crown prince Jung Jung Bahadur was thrown into a quake when he heard the word 'Tiger'. That was exactly what did not happen. As soon as he heard it pronounced, the crown prince gave a deep growl. Terrifying words emerged from his lips.

'Let tigers beware!'

This account is only a rumour rife in Pratibandapuram. But with hindsight we may conclude it was based on some truth.

## 2

Crown prince Jung Jung Bahadur grew taller and stronger day by day. No other miracle marked his childhood days apart from the event already described. The boy drank the milk of an English cow, was brought up by an English nanny, tutored in English by an Englishman, saw nothing but English films—exactly as the crown princes of all the other Indian States did. When he came of age at twenty, the State, which had been with the Court of Wards until then, came into his hands.

But everyone in the kingdom remembered the astrologer's

prediction. Many continued to discuss the matter. Slowly it came to the Maharaja's ears.

There were innumerable forests in the Pratibandapuram State. They had tigers in them. The Maharaja knew the old saying, 'You may kill even a cow in self-defence'. There could certainly be no objection to killing tigers in self-defence. The Maharaja started out on a tiger hunt.

The Maharaja was thrilled beyond measure when he killed his first tiger. He sent for the State astrologer and showed him the dead beast.

'What do you say now?' he demanded.

'Your majesty may kill ninety-nine tigers in exactly the same manner. But . . .' the astrologer drawled.

'But what? Speak without fear.'

'But you must be very careful with the hundredth tiger.'

'What if the hundredth tiger were also killed?'

'Then I will tear up all my books on astrology, set fire to them, and . . .'

'And . . .'

'I shall cut off my tuft, crop my hair short and become an insurance agent,' the astrologer finished on an incoherent note.

3

From that day onwards it was celebration time for all the tigers inhabiting Pratibandapuram.

The State banned tiger hunting by anyone except the Maharaja. A proclamation was issued to the effect that if anyone dared to fling so much as a stone at a tiger, all his wealth and property would be confiscated.

The Maharaja vowed he would attend to all other matters only after killing the hundred tigers. Initially the king seemed well set to realize his ambition.

Not that he faced no dangers. There were times when the bullet missed its mark, the tiger leapt upon him and he fought the beast with his bare hands. Each time it was the Maharaja who won.

At another time he was in danger of losing his throne. A high-ranking British officer visited Pratibandapuram. He was very fond of hunting tigers. And fonder of being photographed with the tigers he had shot. As usual, he wished to hunt tigers in Pratibandapuram. But the Maharaja was firm in his resolve. He refused permission. 'I can organize any other hunt. You may go on a boar hunt. You may conduct a mouse hunt. We are ready for a mosquito hunt. But tiger hunt! That's impossible!'

The British officer's secretary sent word to the Maharaja through the dewan that the durai himself did not have to kill the tiger. The Maharaja could do the actual killing. What was important to the durai was a photograph of himself holding the gun and standing over the tiger's carcass. But the Maharaja would not agree even to this proposal. If he relented now, what would he do if other British officers turned up for tiger hunts?

Because he prevented a British officer from fulfilling his desire, the Maharaja stood in danger of losing his kingdom itself.

The Maharaja and the dewan held deliberations over this issue. As a result, a telegram was despatched forthwith to a famous British company of jewellers in Calcutta. 'Send samples of expensive diamond rings of different designs.'

Some fifty rings arrived. The Maharaja sent the whole lot to the British officer's good lady. The king and the minister expected the duraisani to choose one or two rings and send the rest back. Within no time at all the duraisani sent her reply: 'Thank you very much for your gifts.'

In two days a bill for three lakhs of rupees came from the British jewellers. The Maharaja was happy that though he had lost three lakhs of rupees, he had managed to retain his kingdom.

4

The Maharaja's tiger hunts continued to be highly successful. Within ten years he was able to kill seventy tigers. And then, an unforeseen hurdle brought his mission to a standstill. The tiger population became extinct in the forests of

Pratibandapuram. Who knows whether the tigers practised birth control or committed harakiri? Or simply ran away from the State because they desired to be shot by British hands alone?

One day the Maharaja sent for the dewan. 'Dewan saheb, aren't you aware of the fact that thirty tigers still remain to be shot down by this gun of mine?' he asked brandishing his gun.

Shuddering at the sight of the gun, the Dewan cried out, 'Your Majesty! I am not a tiger!'

'Which idiot would call you a tiger?'

'No, and I'm not a gun!'

'You are neither tiger nor gun. Dewan saheb, I summoned you here for a different purpose. I have decided to get married.'

The dewan began to babble even more. 'Your Majesty, I have two wives already. If I marry you . . .'

'Don't talk nonsense! Why should I marry you? What I want is a tiger . . .'

'Your Majesty! Please think it over. Your ancestors were married to the sword. If you like, marry the gun. A Tiger King is more than enough for this state. It doesn't need a Tiger Queen as well!'

The Maharaja gave a loud crack of laughter. 'I'm not thinking of marrying either a tiger or a gun, but a girl from the ranks of human beings. First you may draw up statistics of tiger populations in the different native states. Next you may investigate if there is a girl I can marry in the royal family of a state with a large tiger population.'

The dewan followed his orders. He found the right girl from a state which possessed a large number of tigers.

Maharaja Jung Jung Bahadur killed five or six tigers each time he visited his father-in-law. In this manner, ninety-nine tiger skins adorned the walls of the reception hall in the Pratibandapuram palace.

## 5

The Maharaja's anxiety reached a fever pitch when there remained just one tiger to achieve his tally of a hundred. He had this one thought during the day and the same dream at night. By this time the tiger farms had run dry even in his father-in-law's kingdom. It became impossible to locate tigers anywhere. Yet only one more was needed. If he could kill just that one single beast, the Maharaja would have no fears left. He could give up tiger hunting altogether.

But he had to be extremely careful with that last tiger. What had the late chief astrologer said? 'Even after killing ninety-nine tigers the Maharaja should beware of the hundredth . . .' True enough. The tiger was a savage beast after all. One had to be wary of it. But where was that hundredth tiger to be found? It seemed easier to find tiger's milk than a live tiger.

Thus the Maharaja was sunk in gloom. But soon came the happy news which dispelled that gloom. In his own state sheep began to disappear frequently from a hillside village.

It was first ascertained that this was not the work of Khader Mian Saheb or Virasami Naicker, both famed for their ability to swallow sheep whole. Surely, a tiger was at work. The villagers ran to inform the Maharaja. The Maharaja announced a three-year exemption from all taxes for that village and set out on the hunt at once.

The tiger was not easily found. It seemed as if it had wantonly hid itself in order to flout the Maharaja's will.

The Maharaja was equally determined. He refused to leave the forest until the tiger was found. As the days passed the Maharaja's fury and obstinacy mounted alarmingly. Many officers lost their jobs.

One day when his rage was at its height, the Maharaja called the dewan and ordered him to double the land tax forthwith.

'The people will become discontented. Then our state too will fall a prey to the Indian National Congress.'

'In that case you may resign from your post,' said the king.

The dewan went home convinced that if the Maharaja did not find the tiger soon, the results could be catastrophic.

He felt life returning to him only when he saw the tiger which had been brought from the People's Park in Madras and kept hidden in his house.

At midnight when the town slept in peace, the dewan and his aged wife dragged the tiger to the car and shoved it into the seat. The dewan himself drove the car straight to the forest where the Maharaja was hunting. When they reached the forest the tiger launched its satyagraha and refused to get out of the car. The dewan was thoroughly exhausted in his efforts to haul the beast out of the car and push it down to the ground.

On the following day, the same old tiger wandered into the Maharaja's presence and stood as if in humble supplication, 'Master, what do you command of me?' It was with boundless joy that the Majaraja took careful aim at the beast. The tiger fell in a crumpled heap.

'I have killed the hundredth tiger. My vow has been fulfilled,' the Maharaja was overcome with elation. Ordering the tiger to be brought to the capital in grand procession, the Maharaja hastened away in his car.

After the Maharaja left, the hunters went to take a closer look at the tiger. The tiger looked back at them rolling its eyes in bafflement. The men realized that the tiger was not dead; the bullet had missed it. It had fainted from the shock of the bullet whizzing past. The hunters wondered what they should do. They decided that the Maharaja must not come to know that he had missed his target. If he did, they could lose their jobs. One of the hunters took aim from a distance of one foot and shot the tiger. This time he killed it without missing his mark.

Then, as commanded by the king, the dead tiger was taken in procession through the town and buried. A tomb was erected over it.

A few days later the Maharaja's son's third birthday was celebrated. Until then the Maharaja had given his entire mind over to tiger hunting. He had had no time to spare for the crown prince. But now the king turned his attention to the child. He wished to give him some special gift on his birthday. He went to the shopping centre in Pratibandapuram and searched every shop, but couldn't find anything suitable. Finally he spotted a wooden tiger in a toyshop and decided it was the perfect gift.

The wooden tiger cost only two annas and a quarter. But the shopkeeper knew that if he quoted such a low price to the Maharaja, he would be punished under the rules of the Emergency. So, he said, 'Your Majesty, this is an extremely rare example of craftsmanship. A bargain at three hundred rupees!'

'Very good. Let this be your offering to the crown prince on his birthday,' said the king and took it away with him.

On that day father and son played with that tiny little

wooden tiger. It had been carved by an unskilled carpenter. Its surface was rough; tiny slivers of wood stood up like quills all over it. One of those slivers pierced the Maharaja's right hand. He pulled it out with his left hand and continued to play with the prince.

The next day, infection flared in the Maharaja's right hand. In four days, it developed into a suppurating sore which spread all over the arm.

Three famous surgeons were brought in from Madras. After holding a consultation they decided to operate. The operation took place.

The three surgeons who performed it came out of the theatre and announced, 'The operation was successful. The Maharaja is dead.'

In this manner the hundredth tiger took its final revenge upon the Tiger King.

# SIVAKOZHUNDU OF TIRUVAZHUNDUR

'Tiruvazhundur Sivakozhundu'
*Ananda Vikatan* (1939)

# 1

$\mathcal{T}$he train came to a halt at Iyampettai station at exactly 8.30 p.m. A lightning flash illuminated the station, the platform and the thick trees beyond. The darkness now seemed ten times deeper. The flickering light of the station lantern underscored that darkness. 'Who are you to challenge me?' the night seemed to ask as it came rolling down to smother the lantern's existence.

The mere act of boarding a train is enough for some people to be overcome by sleep. The rhythmic movement of the train lulls them at once. But sleep forsakes me on trains. Moreover, how could I hope to sleep on so stormy a night? I worried about having to get through the whole of that night on the train.

I picked up a book and tried to read. It was not easy to read on a moving train. Therefore when I heard the porter shout, 'Iyampettai! Iyampettai!' I opened the shutters and looked out. I remembered that Iyampettai was Kandappan's hometown.

No, you would not have heard of Iyampettai Kandappan, because I have changed his name and hometown. The famous artist was often described as the avatar of Lord Nandi. In his hands the tavil did not sound like an ordinary instrument but became the dundubhi of the gods. Pudukkottai Dakshinamurti Pillai happened to hear him play once, so the legend goes, and flung his own mridangam and kanjira away. For six months after that, he would not even touch a percussion instrument. Iyampettai Kandappan was indeed a peerless exponent of his art. Besides, he always wore khadi and was deeply interested in the nationalist movement. I met him frequently at the sessions of the Congress Party. I had also learnt that he was a fascinating conversationalist. That was why I remembered him and thought that the night would pass easily if he chanced to board the same train that day.

Even as the thought occurred to me, I saw two or three men walking hurriedly towards the train. I looked intently to see if I could recognize them. Why, the first one was Tavil Kandappan himself!

The door to my compartment opened before I could get over my surprise. Kandappa Pillai got in. His companions brought in his luggage: a trunk, his bedroll, and two tavils.

'Has anything been left behind?'

'Everything is here.'

'Check once again and get going.'

'We'll take our leave of you now.'

'Run! Run! Get into the next compartment. Don't go off to sleep and miss the Vizhupuram station, understand?'

The train began to move. The station lantern disappeared from view. The train picked up speed as it tore through the forests of the night.

'Kandappa Pillai! How are you?' I asked.

Surprised, Kandappa Pillai turned to look at me and said, 'Oh, it's you, swami! I am fine. And very happy to see you.'

'I am extremely happy too, to see you. What a coincidence! I thought of you when the train stopped at Iyampettai. I also thought it would be wonderful if you happened to board the train. The next instant brought you right into my compartment! If I tell my friends about this in Madras tomorrow, they won't believe me. They will say it is against nature!'

'Against which nature, swami?' Kandappa Pillai enquired.

'What a question! What do you mean "against which nature"?'

'Look, swami! Take this train now. It is natural for a train to run on its tracks. We get into a train because we believe that it will do that. But once in a while the train runs off the rails, and there's an accident. Those who don't actually witness such a happening can say, "No train will run off the rails, it is unnatural for it to do so".'

Before I could think of an answer, he went on, 'Listen, You can hear the thunder. Ten cracks in the last five minutes. The thunderstorm is a constant phenomenon, raging alternately over some part of the world or the other. Can a single man or creature escape death if all that charge of lightning strikes the earth? No. And therefore it is natural

101

for thunder to crash, and only in the skies. But once in a long while lightning does strike the earth. Then, instead of killing its victim outright, it snatches his eyes away. Swami, would you say this is a natural phenomenon, or that it is against nature?'

We looked at each other. I didn't know what to say.

'Why are you silent, swami? Answer me. If it is natural for lightning to strike the earth, why doesn't it strike each and every one of us? Why does it not blind us all? If it is unnatural for it to strike the earth, how can it strike only a certain individual? And destroy his eyesight? Can this happen? If it cannot happen, how then did it happen?'

I began to wonder if Kandappa Pillai had all his wits about him. Prohibition had not been enforced in Tanjavur, I recalled. Perhaps . . . Was it possible that . . . ? I chided myself for my suspicions. He headed the Congress Committee in his hometown. With a Gandhi cap on his head, he had picketed liquor shops. Could such a person have imbibed liquor? Certainly not.

Then why was he talking nonsense? Why did he babble on and on about thunder and lightning?

In order to change the subject, I asked him, 'Are you coming to town? For a concert perhaps? A wedding concert?'

'Yes, swami. There is a concert in town tomorrow.' With that he picked up his tavil and placed it by his side. He removed the cover and stroked both heads of the drum, as loving as a mother's hands caressing the cheeks of her beloved child.

What was this? Was the man going to stage a solo tavil concert on the train? Just the right thing to induce sleep! As I laughed to myself, he said, 'Swami, I have played the tavil every day, all my life. I have accompanied several great nadaswaram artists. But last night's playing was a bliss altogether different! What amazing sounds were produced on these heads of hide! Was it I who played the instrument? Not at all. Lord Nandi manifested himself in my fingers!'

My interest quickened. I realized then that what had seemed like nonsense a few minutes ago was the excitement of the previous night's inspired performance.

'And where did such a fine concert take place? Who played the nadaswaram?' I asked him.

'Swami, have you heard of Tiruvazhundur Sivakozhundu?'

'Tiruvazhundur Sivakozhundu? Who is he? I haven't hard of him!' I replied. I had heard of an old, famous nadaswaram player called Sivakozhundu, but he had died before I was born. Nor did he belong to Tiruvazhundur.

'No? Think again! Where were you in 1929–30?'

'I see, 1929–30? I spent half of that period as a guest of the government, and the other half at a village far from the railway station at Salem.'

103

'I see, that's why you didn't hear of him. Sivakozhundu Tambi was famous during just those two years. But in those two years, he conquered the entire world of music.'

I felt a sudden stab of pain. 'Isn't it true that some geniuses in the world of art have died early?' I thought at once of Kittappa.

'No, swami, no! Don't even say such a thing! Pray that Tambi may lead a long life!'

'I will be happy to say that! May he live a long and happy life. But why has he been forgotten? Why has he stopped playing?'

'Because the world cannot bear it anymore. It will drive everyone mad. That is why I don't go too often myself to see Tambi. I heard him play last night. Since then I have been gripped by a frenzy. I want to tear my tavil apart and take an oath that I will forswear accompanying anyone else. What an Ataana he played last night! First I had tears in my eyes. Then I wanted to get up and dance in ecstasy. Even now, when I think of it, my hair stands on end!'

## 2

I urged him to tell me everything from the very beginning. Kandappa Pillai began his story:

'It is over twelve years since I first met Sivakozhundu Tambi. He was then just beginning to grow famous. I was

104

asked to accompany him at a concert for a temple ceremony. At first I tried to excuse myself because I thought it was beneath me to accompany a youngster. But those who came to invite me would not let me off. It seems Sivakozhundu Pillai had insisted that I be his tavil accompanist. That made me curious enough to accept and to take an advance from them.

'Judging by the fame he had earned in just two years of concert performance, I expected that he would not play badly. But when Tambi placed the nadaswaram to his lips and began to blow, I realized that this was no mere skill but extraordinary talent. Within half an hour of Tambi's playing I was transported. I was convinced that the boy was a true heir to the heritage of stalwarts like Mannarkudi Chinna Pakkiri and Sembonnarkoil Ramasami.

'I also learnt the reason for Tambi's insistence that I accompany him. While he was apparently extremely fond of my tavil playing, he had another reason as well. For a while, the jealousy of fellow nadaswaram artists had caused every concert of Sivakozhundu's to end in quarrels.

'Swami! Fame is an evil thing. The more it grows, the greater the envy it fosters, especially in the world of art and scholarship. People hate to see a youngster achieve excellence and popularity. Wherever they gathered, it had become the norm for nadaswaram players to disparage Tambi.

105

'Just a month before we met, Sivakozhundu had been invited to perform at a well-known temple, during the festival in the month of Panguni.

'A local nadaswaram artist had also been also engaged for the festival. Animosities mounted between the groups. During the Tirukalyana ritual, as Tambi played in the temple hall, these local musicians sat at the rear and made fun of him. One said, "Those who don't even know how to hold the instrument have come now to perform on stage." Another added, "If listeners be idiots, anyone can perform on stage." Though Sivakozhundu was not oblivious to the claque, he continued to play without paying it any attention. But he lost his temper when a local tavil player accused him of not maintaining the right rhythm. "Who says my talam is wrong? Come forward and show me where I am wrong," he said. There were many admirers of Tambi seated up front and one of them interposed, "Forget these useless chaps. What do they know about music? They only know how to sing for their supper! Go on, play!"

'That was enough to start a fight. The local nadaswaram player brandished his instrument. The tavil players hit one another. Cymbals were grabbed and flung away. All was mayhem for a while. The priest and the temple warden intervened to restore peace after which they conducted an investigation. There were supporters for both sides. The warden was on the side of the jingoistic supporters of the local artist. He declared that Sivakozhundu was the offender, ordered him to stop playing and get out. The priest however, was Tambi's ardent fan. He announced fiercely that if Sivakozhundu left the temple, he would accompany him! This led to more efforts at reconciliation.

'Such incidents occurred not once or twice, but several times. That was the reason why Sivakozhundu decided to get me to be his regular tavil accompanist. Tambi was sure that with me around, no one would dare to make mischief.

'I learnt all this from Tambi himself, much later. Thenceforward, we began always to appear together at concerts. Because of that, I incurred the rancour of the other nadaswaram artists. They even decided to ban me from their groups. I dismissed them as beneath my contempt. But what did I care, swami? My wants are few. The Lord has given me enough for my needs.

'The ban did not affect us at all. Every day brought us a concert. And day by day Tambi's skill grew more and more refined. Earlier, I had played the tavil for money. When I started to play for Tambi, I forgot myself and played in a state of bliss. Swami! What improvisation! What imagination! What creative content! And for all that Tambi never crossed the boundaries of tradition as practised by the elders. He didn't use a tambura instead of the otthu as they do nowadays. Nor did he have the tabla instead of the tavil, or the harmonium and morsing as accompaniments.

I interposed at this point to say, 'Pillai! About the tambura . . .'

But he wouldn't let me go on. 'I know, swami, I know that you are a supporter of the tambura. Let's not go into that issue now. All I'm saying is that Tiruvazhundur Tambi did not take those routes. And yet his music was a miracle. It was the music of the gods . . . truly of the gods . . . It won him greater and greater adulation. The money started pouring in.

'I was extremely happy, except for one thing. Swami, you know that wretched foe of art and artists! Tambi too was a victim of drink. Fiercely determined to free him from the habit, I made indirect allusions to it. I also spoke to him directly about it. Tambi had great respect for me. He would listen quietly without answering back. Not that he didn't know it was a vile addiction. But he was unable to give it up. I consoled myself that my constant advice at least kept it under some control.

'Around that time Mahatma Gandhi launched his salt satyagraha. All of India was in a state of turmoil. You know that I have long been interested in the national movement. I attended several public meetings at that time. Sometimes I took Tambi with me. I realised that Tambi's heart was

108

moved by the speeches of the leaders. Finally, we received the news of Gandhi's arrest. That day it seemed as if the whole of Kumbakonam had turned out for the massive public meeting. Sivakozhundu had made his home in Kumbakonam some two years earlier. I too went there often. Both of us attended that meeting. Everyone spoke with deep feeling that day. I saw tears rolling down from Tambi's eyes.

'An hour passed and then there was a sudden furore. The police were spotted at a little distance, advancing towards the crowd with lathis. On that very day, orders had been received to disperse all public meetings by lathi-charge. The crowd was unaware of this. Before most of them could turn around to see what was happening, the police rushed into the crowd and began to beat up the people ruthlessly. At once the crowd began to disperse. Within a minute or two most of the people ran away. I was one of those who remained till the end. I didn't run. I made my unhurried exit only after receiving four or five hard strokes.

'Tambi had run away early and was waiting for me at a street corner. When he saw me he hugged me and wept. We spoke little as we walked home. On the way, when we came to the Hanuman temple on the market street, Tambi shouted for me to stop and fell full length before the sanctum.

'"Swami! Anjaneya! I swear that from today I will never look on liquor or touch it with my hand!" he vowed.

'Idiot that I was, couldn't I keep my mouth shut? "Tambi! Hanuman is the great god of this age of Kali. And the market street Hanuman is very powerful. You have taken an oath in his presence. Be careful! Don't forget!" said I.

'Then Tambi stated in a loud voice, "If I break my oath, may lightning strike my head and blind me!"

'Swami! I tell you truly, my body trembled and my hair stood on end. I wanted to shout, "Damn you, why did you take such a horrendous oath?" But my tongue cleaved to the roof of my mouth.

## 3

'There was yet another reason for my growing attachment to Sivakozhundu. One of my sisters lived in Puduchetti Street in Kumbakonam. I used to stay with her whenever I went to Kumbakonam. I was as fond of her daughter Vanajakshi as if she were my own child. Sundara Kamakshi and I had decided to get her married into a good family, and not let her enter this shameful profession.

'Sivakozhundu visited me often in Kumbakonam. Then I would think how wonderful it would be if Vanaja were to marry Sivakozhundu. There were signs to show that my wish might come true, signs of a mutual affection growing between them.

'Vanaja did not have the looks of a celestial nymph. Nor

was she bad-looking, for that matter. There was a certain charm about her, and looks that suggested a nice, home-loving girl. But I have never come across a more intelligent girl. Don't think I say this because she is my niece. I have my own children. Do I praise them? Never.

'We had no intention of preparing Vanaja for a career in music or dance. We wanted our profession to end with us, so that our children could be settled in good families. Therefore we sent Vanaja to school. After the seventh or eighth class, we stopped her schooling. Vanaja stayed at home.

'All our efforts could not wipe out a genetic predisposition, an aptitude for the family tradition. Music, dance and acting came easily to the girl and found expression in mischief. She could imitate any singer. If she saw a play she would enact the whole of it, imitating each character perfectly. She could mimic the gait and mannerisms of every one she met, and she would put that skill to comic use. Vanaja was always the centre of fun and laughter. She was afraid of no one and spoke about everyone with nonchalant scorn. I often advised her that this was wrong; she had to be more maidenly and modest.

'But all that mischief, impertinence, laughter and playfulness vanished in the presence of one man. If Sivakozhundu Tambi dropped in, she would suddenly turn shy and modest. She would not raise her voice. She would speak only when she was spoken to. Tambi's jokes would

111

elicit not her usual cracks of laughter, but only a slight smile. She was a keen admirer of Tambi's nadaswaram. She never missed Tambi when he played in Kumbakonam, be it at a festival or a procession. The next time he came, she would remark that a particular ragam was excellent, or that a certain song was a rare piece.

'Whenever I paid them a visit, she would look eagerly to see if Tambi accompanied me. If he did not come, she would ask indirectly if he was in good health.

'I saw that Sivakozhundu's heart was in a similar state. His eyes would search for Vanaja if she was not at the door to welcome him when he came. So was it when he took his leave. He would not leave without bidding her farewell. "Shall we go?" he would ask, but make no move to get up.

'The feelings of the youngsters were no mystery to me. I decided that their bonding was the will óf God. I cannot tell you how happy it made me. My sister was equally content.

'As we rejoiced over our wishes being fulfilled so easily, a witch arrived to dash cold water over our dreams. You will certainly recognize her name. It was Tiruchendur Manoranjitam. Today she is almost forgotten, but my goodness, it is impossible to describe the crazy following she enjoyed in those days. Within ten days of the arrival of her drama company in Kumbakonam, it seemed the whole town had run mad.

112

'Sometimes it is impossible to understand why someone becomes a celebrity in the world of art. My opinion is that Manoranjitam had very mediocre attributes. Of course, at night, when she came and stood before the electric lights with a thickly-powdered face and a silver-spangled saree, she did seem to be out of the ordinary. In daylight, without all that make-up, her face wasn't even as pleasing as mine!

'Her music was simply dreadful. She crooned glittering Hindustani drama melodies. That's about all. Her voice was not bad. But ask her to sing Khambhoji for fifteen minutes! Zero. Ask her to sing a Tyagaraja kriti to perfect time. Impossible! She was the sort who would say, "I haven't brought my sense of rhythm with me, I left it at home today."

'It was over this unremarkable woman that Kumbakonam went mad. One day when the tickets were sold out, people threw stones at the drama pandal. Imagine the size of the thronging crowds! And wherever the woman went during the day, a thousand people followed her. Her visit to the temple attracted crowds as if for a festival. Everyone would gaze at the actress, not at God!

'I was not surprised by this frenzied adulation. I have seen it all so many times since the days of Balamani. But what did surprise me was that Tiruvazhundur Tambi too fell a prey to this craze. There was no end to my anguish. Could there be a greater shame than for a musician of Tambi's genius, proficiency and standing, to fall at the feet of an actress in a drama company!

## 4

'From the day the drama company arrived in Kumbakonam, Sivakozhundu didn't miss a single show. Even if he had to go out of town for some concert, he made sure he got back for the night show.

'Tambi's antics when Manoranjitam came on stage were dreadful to behold.

'And just listen to this joke! The same theatre craze infected Vanajakshi as well. She too attended the shows with unfailing regularity. But I didn't think the play was the only thing which drew her. I noticed this on two or three occasions. While Sivakozhundu gazed at the stage, Vanajakshi's gaze was rivetted on Sivakozhundu. Somehow her eyes would find him even if they were at the opposite ends of the hall.

'I didn't like any of these developments. I could well understand Vanajakshi's state of mind. I saw how her heart constantly ached for him. Sivakozhundu had stopped visiting us. Sometimes, with tears in her eyes, Vanajakshi would ask, "Mama! When is the drama company leaving town?" I understood what that implied. And though I too was upset, I would say, "Silly girl! Why do you worry? What is it to you what other people do? Go and see if there is any work round the house!" At other times she would say, "Mama! I too am going to join the drama company." Then she would proceed to sing all the songs and mime everything Monaranjitam did on stage. Ayyo! This girl has gone absolutely crazy! I would say to myself and feel very sorry.

'You know how our people are given to wild exaggeration, dealing in mere fibs and fabrications. What then do you expect when there is a certain amount of truth involved in the matter? The whole town gossiped about Sivakozhundu's infatuation. I was sad that a man of genius should have acquired the reputation of an idiot.

'At last the play drew to a close. That is, the drama company's engagement at Kumbakonam came to an end. Their next destination was Madras. We came to know that the day they left, Sivakozhundu went to their quarters, stayed there, and behaved in an extremely foolish manner. He also went to the railway station to see them off. To the amusement of everyone on the platform, when the train began to move, Sivakozhundu shouted, "I will definitely come and see you in the city!"

'Vanaja perked up a little when the drama company had left town. "Mama! Sivakozhundu Tambi will start visiting us again, won't he?" she asked. Just as she expected, he did visit us once or twice. You should have seen Vanaja during those times! My goodness, she behaved like an imperious queen! She would walk up and down but never once did her eyes meet Sivakozhundu's. If he did say something, she wouldn't respond, pretending not to hear him.

'All this both amused and saddened me. No, swami! I gave them no advice. I have learnt from experience that in the affairs of young people, all advice is absolutely useless. That is why I had held my tongue even when Sivakozhundu had been ensnared by that actress. People have to face disappointments and mature by their own experience. They have to live through their own joys and sorrows to become wise. Any interference only worsens matters.

'Some three months passed. I received a letter asking me to bring Sivakozhundu to the Kandaswami temple festival in Madras. I did recall that the dreadful woman was in the city. But how could we turn down the engagement? We went. Swami, Sivakozhundu simply excelled himself at that festival! By some intuition, Tambi must have realized that these were to be his last public concerts. Perhaps that was why it turned out to be so outstanding a performance. In one of the concerts, Tambi's Bhairavi made the listeners weep.

'His style had changed in some ways. Earlier, his zest had been reserved for ragams like Kalyani, Sankarabharanam, Hamsadhvani, Nattai and Kedaram. They made me play the tavil with great enthusiasm. But more recently, Tambi had taken to playing ragams like Khambhoji, Kedaragowlai, Huseni, Mukhari, and Khamas. As I played with him, I would find my eyes filling with tears. I would get goose-flesh. I would cease to think about playing the tavil. My hands tapped on out of long habit, but my mind would be completely lost in Tambi's music. At times I simply raised my folded hands to cry out, "Hara hara Mahadeva!" Some people giggled at this. Fools! What did they know of the taste of music?

'The three days of concerts were over. On the morning of the fourth day I asked Tambi, "Shall we leave today?"

'"Wait, Mama! Our concert at Chidambaram is only on Wednesday. Let's drive down by car."

'Driving was Sivakozhundu's latest craze. Having learnt to drive, he had been saying that the next time he went to Madras, he was going to buy a car.

'After a whole day's search he did return with a second-hand car purchased for two thousand rupees. Sparingly used, it was in very good condition.

'Thank God, the pursuit of the car had made him forget Manoranjitam, or so I happily imagined. But my joy was short-lived. Sivakozhundu went to see the play that night, half-heartedly inviting me to accompany him. "Not me, I am tired," I replied. I spent the whole night in misery.

'The next day Tambi got up very late. Hardly was he up before he began to get ready with a palpable excitement.

117

Dressed nattily, he told me, "Mama! I am going out. Don't wait for me to join you for lunch. I may be late."

'I said, "Tambi, what is this! We must be in Chidambaram at daybreak tomorrow. And you are going out without making any arrangements for the journey!"

'"We will definitely start tonight, Mama!' he said. "If we leave by car at 10 p.m., we will be in Chidambaram early in the morning. If you want a good night's sleep, you take the night train."

'I expected him back only in the evening, and was surprised that he returned within the hour. He did not answer my queries but went straight up to bed and lay there. I heard his sobs.

'The chokra boy had accompanied him. So I asked him what had happened. He gave me all the details. When they went to Manoranjitam's bungalow in San Thome, there were already six cars outside her home. Tambi sent word that Sivakozhundu Pillai had come from Kumbakonam to see her. The watchman returned to say that since "Amma" was busy and wouldn't be able to see him, he should come later. Tambi's face shrank in shame. He returned to our quarters at once.

'Swami! I was not surprised. I had heard that the people of Madras had spread the red carpet out for that woman. Eminent advocates, high court judges and I.C.S. officers went to her home and waited for an audience! This kind of

118

celebrity can turn the head of even virtuous persons. What
do you expect from a wretched woman? Why will she waste
time on a poor nadaswaram player?

'I was angry with Sivakozhundu as well. A man with his
depth of musicial talent going in search of a worthless chit!
He certainly deserved this humiliation. Only then will he
learn his lesson. Well, let him weep!

'Feeling as I did, I didn't try to console him. I went out
because I had some people to see.

'I returned around five o'clock and enquired about Tambi.
I learnt that Tambi had come out of his room at four o'clock,
asked for me, and then left in his car. At first I thought of
taking the train and leaving him to find his way. Then I felt
that he should not be abandoned in that condition. I grew
extremely uneasy. If by some chance, Tambi did not return,
what about the concert at Chidambaram? I told myself that
his irresponsible behaviour was no excuse for any silliness
on my part. So I waited for him.

'The car returned only at 7 p.m.

'"So you are back, Mama!" When Sivakozhundu entered
the room merrily, I was happy to think that he was himself
again. But that happiness was short-lived. At once I knew
the reason for his high spirits. I was shattered.

'"Slut! This mishap is all due to you!" I cursed the actress.
I also cursed myself for having left Tambi alone that evening.

It was now too late to think of my going by train. I had to make sure that Tambi came with me.'

At this juncture I couldn't quite make out what Kandappa Pillai said. I felt that he had left out something. 'I don't understand, Ayya! What change did you note in Sivakozhundu?' I asked him.

'Don't you understand, swami! I feel bad to spell it out. The boy was heavily drunk. That's all. The oath at the Hanuman temple was broken. Once again I asked the chokra boy for details. He told me that they had gone once again to the actress' house and received the same reply. As they stood outside the gate they saw her come out, get into a car and drive away, without a backward glance at Tambi. After that Tambi drove all over the place for a while and finally ended up somewhere near the Central Station. The hellborn have opened liquor shops everywhere. Tambi had got thoroughly drunk.

'When I heard this account, though I was angry with the man, I also felt sorry for him. How deep must have been the hurt which made him disregard a vow taken in a temple! How amazing is the power of the passion for a woman! But I consoled myself with the thought, never mind, if I managed to take him home safely this once, I wouldn't have to worry any more. He is free of his craze for the actress now. It is up to Vanaja now to take care of him.

120

# 5

'It was 10 p.m. by the time we finished dinner and got ready to leave. The car dealer had sent a chauffeur. Sivakozhundu was seated in front beside the driver. We were all at the back. I was afraid that Tambi would want to drive himself. I didn't speak to him about it because it might put the idea into his head. So I kept my mouth shut.

'The sky was overcast. But when we set out on our journey, it didn't look as if it would rain. It began to drizzle when we passed Chengalpattu. I looked at the sky. It was totally black. I feared that it might rain heavily.

'I must have dozed off with that thought. I don't know how long I slept. I was startled awake by a tremendous clap of thunder.

'In all my life, I had never seen such a storm. The thunder began to explode in one corner of the sky, tore through the clouds as it travelled to another. Nor did it travel fast. It made the spheres in space tremble in terror as it moved at its measured pace. Simultaneously, the light of a thousand suns blazed in a single flash of lightning. It paused in the sky for half a minute to light up the whole world. My dazzled eyes shut themselves. But before they did I saw something that hit me with horror in the pit of my stomach. Swami, Sivakozhundu was in the driver's seat!

121

'Ayyo! Lightning flashed within me warning me of disaster. And disaster struck.

'How can I describe what happened in that single instant? There was a horrendous blast. I had never heard such a sound in this life of mine, nor will I hear it again. How do you think it feels when the whole sky crashes over your head? That's what I felt had happened. For an instant I became deaf. The next instant brought a massive shock, as if I was flung from the earth into the underworld.

'As long as I live, I will never forget what I saw when I came to. A huge green banyan tree before me was in flames. Picture the sight! In the colossal blackness of the earth and sky, a green tree and a motor car were going up in flames! It was drizzling then. The drops of water falling on the fire and vanishing in the flames, as if the God of Fire was sticking his tongue out again and again to taste the little raindrops, and rising higher and higher towards the clouds as his great thirst could hardly be assuaged by them. For a while I lay where I was, witnessing this terrible sight. Fortunately, I remembered that my tavil was in the car. That revived me. I raced towards the car. It had been smashed against the tree. Luckily only the engine was burning. The fire had not yet reached the boot. Moving the tavil and nadaswaram to safety, I turned to examine the condition of the occupants of the car. The driver had just got up and was coming towards the

122

car. His head was hurt, blood flowing from it. I cursed him soundly for what he had done and looked for Tambi. Seeing him flat on the ground a little ahead, I rushed towards him. He lay inert, like a log. Ayyo! Was the boy dead? I put my hand on his chest. No heart beat. I held his wrist. No pulse. I put my hand on his nostrils. The breath came faintly. I too felt my life return.

'Hearing loud voices I looked around and saw that seven or eight men were approaching us with lanterns. Later I learnt that there was a railway station close by. See the ways of God! Even when he sends us punishment, he shows some mercy. What would have been our fate if this had occurred in a deserted place?'

'Pillaival! What actually happened? Why did the tree catch fire? Why did the car go up in flames?' I asked.

'Don't you see? When does a green tree burn? Only when it is struck by lightning.'

'Ayyo! That oath at the Hanuman temple . . . '

'Yes! Sivakozhundu's words at the temple came true. The shock of lightning striking so close to him must have made Tambi lose his grip on the steering wheel. The car hit the tree. But listen! Miraculously, no one died. All of us escaped with slight bruises. But Tambi . . . Tambi . . . When I think of that, I have to believe that it was divine retribution.

'I couldn't get rid of my fear that he was dead because he

123

continued to lie like a log. I would look at his face to reassure myself that it had some life in it. It was then that I saw something shining in the corner of his eyes. I looked more carefully. My God!

'That was when I felt a spear-thrust tearing my heart apart. In the corner of those closed eyes were drops of blood. Under the electric light they glowed like rubies!

'Four days later, my suspicion was confirmed. I had taken him to the hospital run by the famous doctor who belonged to our Congress party. The doctor did not say anything for the first three days. On the fourth day, he called me and declared simply, "The man is in a state of mental shock. He will recover from this soon. But his eyes are lost forever." I didn't ask why. I knew the reason, didn't I? Tambi's words at the Hanuman temple had come absolutely true. His oath, that lightning should blind him if he touched liquor again, had been fulfilled.

## 6

'Tambi lay in the hospital for three months. Slowly his mind cleared. He recognized me within ten days. His eyes were still bandaged. I couldn't bring myself to tell him that he had lost his eyesight. I told the doctor to tell him about it in my absence. When he knew that he had lost his vision forever, Tambi seemed to lose his wits once again. And yet, in the midst of all these tribulations he did not forget the actress! Often he would smile to himself, and repeat her name. I didn't feel like bringing Vanaja to see him.

'Vanaja, however, was impatient to see him. I put her off by saying that the doctor had forbidden all visitors. Finally, unable to withstand her pestering, I took her to the hospital. We had both decided not to inform Tambi of her visit. Accordingly, she came into the sick room and stood in silence.

'It happened as I feared. As he talked to himself Sivakozhundu called out to Manoranjitam by name and babbled endearments to her. I glanced at Vanaja with great anxiety. Ayya! Haven't the elders said that it is impossible for men to understand the hearts of women? I realized then how true that was. I thought that Vanaja would be disgusted when she saw how Sivakozhundu was still enamoured of Manoranjitam, and lose all her love for him. But what happened was exactly the opposite. Vanaja's feelings did not waver one bit. If anything, her affections seemed to grow deeper.

'She demanded to be taken to the hospital every day, but without my disclosing her identity to Tambi. She insisted on sending food to him daily, and brought it herself on some days. I didn't like any of this. True, I had wanted to give Vanaja in marriage to Sivakozhundu earlier. But was it possible now? Would her mother agree? Would this daft boy

125

ever agree to it? After all that had happened, he had still not got over his infatuation for Manoranjitam! So what was the use encouraging Vanaja's feelings?

'Even as I ruminated, I was disconcerted by something she wanted to do. "Mama! You must agree to my proposal," was the beginning of a long speech which ended with, "I am going to change my name to Manoranjitam. You must give me your consent."

'At first I couldn't make out head or tail of her request. I understood however when Vanaja said that she was going to take advantage of Tambi's blindness and turn herself into Manoranjitam. She told me that she could talk, sing and behave like Manoranjitam, and forthwith proceeded to mimic her perfectly. Her voice and speech were carbon copies of what I had seen on the stage.

'I was not at all in favour of cheating Tambi in this manner. I also feared that it might result in something unpleasant. But I could not withstand Vanaja's obstinacy and tears. "Mama! I have nothing in the world but him. Since he doesn't like Vanaja, I will transform myself into Manoranjitam. You must agree to this. Otherwise I will kill myself and you will be responsible for a woman's death."

'After many days of vacillation, I finally agreed to this deception. I couldn't bear to see the girl's misery. Also there was still hope that if the plot succeeded, Sivakozhundu might

126

return to his former self. At the same time, I was preyed upon by fear and anxiety. First, the plot had to succeed. But how would Tambi react when the truth came out? I finally decided that there was a God in heaven, and let things take their course.

'The next day I took Vanaja to Tambi's house. As I wondered how to bring up the topic, by chance Vanaja's bangles happened to tinkle, catching Tambi by surprise.

'"Who's that, Mama?" he asked.

'With some relief, I answered, "Tambi, Manoranjitam has come to see you from Madras."

'"What! Manoranjitam?" Tambi exclaimed and sat up in bed. For a minute, I was scared.

'But Vanaja came forward at once, and placing her hands on his shoulders she made him lie down again, saying, "Yes it is me. You must rest now."

'Ayyo! Tambi's look of that moment still haunts me. He stared and stared with his sightless eyes. Don't people realize the value of things only when they lose them? Tambi must have realized the value of sight most dearly at that moment. I was pained to see the boundless anguish on his face for those eyes now irrevocably lost. I also felt ashamed for attempting to deceive him. But what was the use of feeling sorry after being persuaded by the girl to comply?

'I told him the story Vanaja and I had concocted earlier.

As if I had learnt it by rote, I said that since he had been calling out to Manoranjitam again and again when he lay unconscious in the hospital, I had written to the woman believing that he would get well only if she came to see him. That had brought her here.

'Vanaja reiterated that she had come running when she saw the letter and that she would return only after he got well.

'After some more talk of this kind I said, "Amma! Sing something for Tambi." We had planned this too in advance.

'One of the roles played by Manoranjitam was that of Nandan. As Nandan, she would sing the arutpa "Padamudiyaadini tuyaram" as a ragamalika. Vanaja now sang the same song in the same manner. I was astounded by her exact imitation of the actress' voice, and style of singing, and her precise reproduction of her embellishments of the melody. Tambi listened in a state of bliss. The tears flowed from his eyes.

'We were both extremely happy that our plot had succeeded so well. Vanaja started to visit Tambi, often spending the whole day with him. Tambi had no close relatives. There was no one in the house except for the cook and the chokra boy. I had prepared them for this plan.

'After a while, I began to accept concert engagements. On my return after one such trip, Sivakozhundu announced

128

joyfully, "Mama! Manoranjitam and I are going to get married. She has decided to give up acting on the stage."

'I became distraught. What a trial! I had agreed to the deception only for the sake of Tambi getting well. How could I agree to this wedding? Can the truth be hidden forever from him? What would happen when he came to know it?

'All these objections had no impact on Vanaja. "It is I who will bear the consequences. Why are you worried?" she argued. Somehow she extracted my consent with her sobs and tears. She made her mother consent as well.

'One month later, we performed their wedding at the Tirunageswarar temple.' With these words, Kandappa Pillai fell silent, as if sunk in deep thought.

'What comes next?' I asked him.

'Well, my nephew and niece are very happy. They have two lovely little boys now.'

I was not satisfied. I felt he had left something unsaid.

'Where are they now?' I asked.

'Have you heard of Mundirisolai, swami? It is on the seashore between Karaikkal and Mutthupettai. The Mariamman temple in Mundirisolai is very famous. It is a beautiful village. Cashew trees and casuarinas grow all around it as far as the eye can see. On the east, beyond the groves, there is a wilderness of reeds. Beyond that, a sea full of waves.

Roaring waves and soughing casuarina are perpetual sounds there.

'Mundirisolai is my native village. I have a small house and some land there. Sivakozhundu had visited this village twice or thrice in the days of his glory. He often used to say he loved the place, and that, if ever he retired from his concert career, he would like to live there.

'A few days after the wedding, Tambi said that he wanted my house in Mundirisolai as he wished to go and live there. I tried to dissuade him. "What does loss of sight matter? That should not make you stop performing. In the past, didn't Sarabha Sastri play the flute though he was blind? Don't worry that you won't be asked to play at concerts. You will have a surfeit of them."

'All that was in vain. He insisted stubbornly, "We will see about all that later. I want to stay in the village for a few years. I don't even want to touch the nadaswaram for a while." That is how he left with Vanaja for Mundirisolai. They are there now.'

7

That was how Kandappa Pillai brought his story to an end for the second time. And yet I was not satisfied. I believed his account of Sivakozhundu's unexpected loss of eyesight because I had witnessed similar unlikely events in my own

130

life. But I simply could not find it credible that Vanaja had transformed herself into Manoranjitam convincingly enough to deceive Sivakozhundu. Was it possible to practice such deceit even on a blind man? Perhaps such deception could succeed before marriage, but was it possible to continue it afterwards?

'So Sivakozhundu never found out that he had been tricked?' I asked.

'Swami! How many nights of sleeplessness do you think I endured because of just this thought? Will Tambi discover the truth? Will he fall into a rage? What will he do? I was never free from these fears. This fear and my love for the couple drew me often to Mundirisolai. I made it a point to visit them at least once in four months. But I was happy to see them leading a very happy life together.

'Once, on such a visit, I saw Tambi's instrument in the main room. I also saw a sruti box beside it. "Does Tambi play the nadaswaram now?" I asked. "Sometimes he plays at night. I accompany him on the drone," Vanaja told me.

'Fortunately I had my tavil with me. That night I insisted that he play the nadaswaram and I accompanied him on the tavil. What an experience that was! Swami, it was not the the music of this earth, but of the spheres. At times you choked, at times you wanted to laugh. Suddenly you were lifted somewhere high into the skies, and then plunged as if

from the top of a mountain to the world below. Sometimes
you felt you were swinging gently, and then you felt impelled
to get up and dance in a frenzy. There were moments when
I stopped playing the tavil and burst into cries of wonder.

'When I realized that Tambi had started playing again, I
began to go more frequently to Mundirisolai. As time passed
my fears diminished. I thought that he would never discover
the truth after all this time.

'Some three or four years after they had settled in
Mundirisolai, on one of my visits, I absent-mindedly called
my niece by her real name. I was panic stricken.

'"Vanaja? Who's that, Mama!" Sivakozhundu asked.

'"There's no Vanaja here, I called out my niece's name
absent-mindedly."

'"Never mind, Mama! My wife is also your niece. If you
like the sound of Vanaja, by all means call her by that name,"
said he.

'I thanked God for the respite.

'That night Sivakozhundu played the nadaswaram as he
usually did. When he played Sahana, I was so overwhelmed
that I cried out the Lord's name in ecstasy. When he finished
I broke down. "Tambi! It is God who is blind. How could
He gift you such genius and snatch your eyes away!"

'That was when Sivakozhundu said with a smile, "Mama!
Truly God did not snatch my eyes from me. In fact, he gave

132

my eyes back to me. Didn't I prefer another woman to
Vanaja? Who could have been more blind?"

'I was completely taken off my guard. "Tambi! What are
you saying?" I said.

'"Mama! You tried to trick me because I was blind. But
it was I who deceived you. I knew her to be Vanaja on the
very first day she came to the hospital," he said.

'Just then Vanaja joined us. From the smile on her face,
I realized that she had colluded with him in this matter.

'"Vanaja! Were you with him in this plot? Did you know
that Tambi knew the truth even before you got married?"

'"No, Mama! I knew it only the day after the wedding.
But he made me promise that I wouldn't tell you. It was his
punishment for your trying to trick him."

'"So you two are together in this! I am the odd man out.
What have I left to stay for? I'm leaving," said I.

'In reality, I was delighted. But I pretended to sulk. With
great difficulty they reconciled me to the situation!

'Once I got over my "anger", I said, "Never mind, Tambi!
But you said you recognized Vanaja from day one. How?"

'Sivakozhundu's answer stunned me utterly.

'"If God takes one sense away, he sharpens another. Yes,
Mama! I lost my eyes, but my ears grew very keen. As soon
as I heard her bangles, I knew it was Vanaja. Besides, I knew
for certain that Manoranjitam would never come. When I

133

was breaking my oath at the Central Station, I heard her drunken laughter in the next room. I was disgusted. Would such a woman come to see me? Certainly not. The real surprise was that you tried to trick me with such a big lie. I guessed the reason for it. You mistook for passion the disgust which made me babble on and on about Manoranjitam. Any doubts I had vanished when Vanaja sang 'Padamudiyadini tuyaram'.

"'Mama! You call yourself a connoisseur? How could you not discern the difference between the tone of the actress and that of your niece? True, the ragam, voice and melodic embellishments were just the same. But there was no soul in Manoranjitam's singing. It was all crooning from the throat. But your niece sang from the depths of her heart. And you couldn't tell the difference!"

'Well, that is how my nephew and niece made a fool of me. But I was not unhappy. I felt a burden slip away from my heart. I wanted the young people to be happy. What have I to worry about? This is the age for cultivating detachment. I have experienced the joys and sorrows of life. I have even felt the celestial bliss of Tambi's music. I am ready to leave when the Lord calls me . . .'

The train came to a halt at Vizhupuram Station. Kandappa Pillai's chokra boy got down from another compartment and came to take his unrolled bed and trunk. Patting the tavil once, Kandappa Pillai picked it up himself

134

and got down. 'Good bye, Ayya! I will see you when I come into the city,' he said and went his way.

I couldn't sleep for the rest of that night. I pondered over the amazing events narrated by Iyampettai Kandappan. Were they true? Or figments of Kandappa Pillai's imagination? I must enquire more into the matter when I see him next and find out the truth.

Well, whether truth or fiction, in one way, the story made me feel content. For, unlike my own stories which end in grief, hadn't he concluded his with the auspicious 'They lived happily ever after'?

# THE BIG
# SWELLING SEA

'Pongumankadal'
*Kalki* (1948)

# 1

*I* don't enjoy the saaral in Kuttralam. People from towns and villages nearby crowd into it and cause a steep fall in the standards of hygiene. If only the British had spent on Kuttralam a hundredth part of the money they spent on Kodaikanal or Ootacamund . . .

Wait . . . Where did I hear that statement? Yes, I remember . . . Didn't I say I avoid Kuttralam in the saaral season? But I used to go there in high summer, when it was uncrowded, and neither damp nor wet. It was easier then to go up the hills, up to Pongumangadal, the big swelling sea.

Beyond that, you reached the marappalam or wooden bridge, and went up to the Shenbaga Devi Falls, even to the Honey Falls in the heights.

Nothing equals the joy of that trek. To climb the hills in the cool morning gives you a pleasure quite unique. Through the gaps between the peaks, the rising sun sends his rays of welcome. Cross over from one hill to another and you see thousands of trees, row after row, each clad in a different green.

The dull roar of the falls and the trills of the birds make a heavenly symphony.

One day I went up the hills, savouring every one of these joys. I intended to go only as far as the Sitraruvi (Little Falls),

139

but the beauty of the slopes drew me on, until I reached the heights of Shenbaga Devi. On the eastern side of the falls there are huge rocks upon which grow tall trees that seem to touch the sky.

The mornings are cool there. Few venture so far. It is the perfect place for the man who wants to be alone.

What joy . . . peace . . . sweet solitude!

But I realized I was mistaken.

'Sujalam-suphalam-malayaja sitalam . . .' An old male voice sang the first line from the anthem 'Vande Mataram'. I turned to see where it came from. In a cleft below, not far from the falls, a sadhu was seated on a flat rock.

He had a long beard and matted locks. His clothes were white, his voice was old, but his hair and beard were jet black.

As I speculated on this paradox, the mendicant saw me. For a while he looked at me. Then he made a sign to say he was coming up. And so he did. Calmly he sat down beside me and took off his beard and wig. And I saw a man of seventy, with hair as white as the tumbai flower. With his deep hollow eyes boring into me, he said, 'This place is ruined. If only the British had spent on Kuttralam a hundredth part of the money they spent on Kodaikanal or Ootacamund, would things have become so bad?'

'Sir, who are you?' I asked.

'What does it matter? Isn't it true, what I said?'

'It is true . . .'

'Then let it be.'

So I did. That is, I stopped talking. But he was not silent.

'I heard you write stories. Is that so?'

I could not hear my answer but his words resounded in my ears.

'Will you write my story?'

I shall fulfil my promise to him.

## 2

The old man with hair as white as the tumbai flower, his broad forehead creased with lines, deep eyes shining with intelligence, and a sharp curved nose, said to me:

'Thirty-five years ago in May 1911, after fruitless wandering in Tirunelveli and Tiruvananthapuram, I came to Kuttralam for the first time. Ramabhadra Sharma of Tiruvananthapuram then lived here in a little bungalow. He was a Moderate. Do you know what that means? He belonged to the political party which included Gopalkrishna Gokhale and Rashbehari Bose. He believed that independence could be obtained by falling at the feet of the white man and begging him for it.

'In those days there were some young hotheads in this region. They went about declaring "Revenge for Bal Gangadhar Tilak!" "Avenge V. O. Chidambaram Pillai!" and

141

"Destroy the white man and fling him into hell, bag and baggage!"

'Ramabhadra Sharma's task was to preach moderation to them. I was eager to meet at least one of those brave and proud young men, but if I tried to get any information about them, Sharma would spread his hands and say he knew nothing. One day he suddenly packed up and went back to his native place. Anyway, having come all the way to Kuttralam, I thought, why not take a look at Shenbaga Devi before I left? So, one day around nine in the morning, I began to trudge up the hill. At one point voices from above fell on my ears. One of them belonged to a young woman. "I was young and innocent, I knew nothing about the world when my aunt and uncle got me married to him. In the early days he too was loving and affectionate. We inherited a bit of land. We could grow paddy there. During the season the gentry would come to bathe in the waterfalls of Kuttralam. We took up housework with one of those families, making sure that they were respectable people. We ate well, we saved some money, twenty or thirty rupees. There was no work in summer. Then we went to fairs and festivals, visited Tiruchendur during the sacred temple procession . . . We went everywhere, saw everything. We lived with such dignity . . ."

'I was surprised to hear such chaste diction from a member of the farming community in Tirunelveli. But what

142

the woman said next startled me into forgetting the purity of her speech.

'"But these freedom fighters came and our family life is ruined. He doesn't work any more. Running to Tuticorin or Tirunelveli or Ettayapuram or Alapuzha has become his job now. Never mind! I can still manage to run my home on my own. But what I cannot understand is his behaviour in the last six months. Like thieves, strangers come in the night and take him away. They bring him back after daybreak. He smears a huge red dot on his forehead. You should listen to his talk. It is weird. 'Sacrifice!' he says. 'Blood!' he says. I am terrified that he might be trapped by the black arts of the Malayali magicians. I have put all my faith in Shenbaga Devi. Every Friday I come to worship her. The goddess alone can save my husband for me!"

'I overtook the speakers and saw that the man was the temple priest, and the woman was about twenty-five years old, tall and slim like the labourers of the Pandya country.

3

'Thirty-five years ago, on a Friday afternoon, here in this very place, sat a sadhu with matted locks. A young woman came to draw water for the ritual bathing of the goddess Shenbaga Devi at the temple. At first she did not see the monk. The sadhu cleared his throat as she bent to fill her

143

pot. The woman looked up and saw him. She approached him with folded hands.

'"Woman, you have great pain in your heart," said the monk.

'"Yes, swami! Only a great soul like you can cure it," the woman said.

'"And we will cure it. Tell me, what is your problem?"

'"Don't you know it? Do you have to learn it from this Ponniyamma's lips?"

'The monk guessed that faith and doubt warred in Ponniyamma's mind.

'"Right. We will tell you. You are worried about your husband. For the past six months his behaviour has not been satisfactory. Doesn't come home at the proper time or even at night. He goes out after dark. He travels from place to place. Doesn't tell you why at times he puts on a huge red kumkumam mark on his forehead. Am I right or wrong?"

'"You are right, swami! You seem to know everything. Swami must save my husband, protect my family!" said the woman with tears in her eyes.

'"All right. I will save you. But you must trust me completely. Let me test you now. Has anyone sought your house in the last two or three days? Brought news for your husband?"

'"Yes, swami! The day before yesterday a man came from

144

Chenkottai. He said that everyone was to meet on the beach at Tuticorin on Sunday, holding a shell in the hand as the sign. I don't know the reason for this. I always have doubts when outsiders come home. Swami, I have told you what I heard when I eavesdropped on them."

'"You have done well. Don't worry any more. Your husband is under the spell of sorcerers from Kerala. I will save him for you. Come and see me here at the same spot next Friday. I will tell you more."

'"Ponniyamma!" came the priest's voice from the temple.

'"I'm coming," Ponniyamma called out.

'The monk looked hard at her and warned, 'Be careful. No one must know what we talked about. Not even the priest. Then everything will go wrong, and you will not get your husband back.'

'On the following Sunday afternoon, I strolled across the sandy beach at Tuticorin. When I saw a man with a shell in his hand, I displayed the shell I held in mine. "Vande mataram!" said he. I repeated the slogan. He looked at me with suspicion and walked away.

'When I greeted two other shell-holders with the same slogan, they responded with "Long live Chidambaram Pillai!" and "Death to the white man!"

'"Where are the others?" I asked them.

'"They are where they should be," one of them answered

145

and moved on. I followed them.

'At last we reached a sheltered hollow where some fifteen men had assembled.

'The man who had met me first and felt suspicious was among them. He said to the man at the centre of the group, "Swami, this newcomer did not know the right response. You must find out who he is."

'The man addressed as "Swami" turned to me. He was young. His face had a natural beauty, enhanced by the glow of yoga sadhana—the practice of austerities. I was dazzled by his keen glance.

'"Fellow, who are you?" he asked.

'It irked me that he should address me with scant respect even though I was much older than him. But I suppressed my irritation to reply, "I have come from Coimbatore. The man from this town who is now there has sent a message."

'You should have seen the palpable excitement in the group. "Really?" "What did he say?" "When did he say it?" They rained questions at me.

'Making a sign for silence, the chief asked me authoritatively, "Sir, you must explain yourself clearly. Many men from this town may be in Coimbatore now. Whom do you mean? What was his message?"

'I guessed that this must be Yogi Neelakantha Brahmachari of Puducheri.

146

'One of the men betrayed agitation. "Is this just by word of mouth? You should check if it is authentic." The man next to him said, "Hush, Vanchi!" From this I inferred that the agitated man was Chenkottai Vanchi Iyer and resolved to be careful with him.

'The chief said again, "Answer my questions."

'My eyes swept over the group as I began to speak in a firm voice.

'"I refer to V.O. Chidambaram Pillai who started a shipping company to compete with the White Man. Who else could I mean? Poor and unworthy as I am, I had the privilege of serving that great soul for a whole year. I was falsely accused of forgery. But I will continue to pray for the blessed men who accused me falsely because they got me sentenced to a term of imprisonment and enabled me to meet this noble son of Mother India. Never have I known anyone as brave, self-sacrificing, honourable and glorious as he. Sir, that extraodinary soul worked on the oil press turning the wheel with his holy hands, doing the work of bulls." Tears came to my eyes as I spoke. I broke off to weep. Some of the others were equally affected. Vanchi Iyer sobbed aloud. Madathukudai Chidambaram Pillai covered his face with a piece of cloth and gave way to grief.

'Vandemataram Subramania Iyer fell upon the earth and cried his heart out. Reputed though he was to possess a heart

147

of stone, Neelakantha Brahmachari's eyes misted over.

'Finally I delivered the message sent by Chidambaram Pillai.

'"Don't worry about me. I am willing to undergo worse tortures for Mother India's deliverance. But my blood boils when I think of the White Man's smug conviction that in jailing Chidambaram Pillai he has suppressed the whole national movement. Don't let history record that the imprisonment of Chidambaram Pillai and Subramania Siva spelt the end of the Swadeshi movement."

'I took out a crumpled piece of paper from the folds of my dhoti at the waist. "Does anyone know Chidambaram Pillai's handwriting?"

'"Yes!" Two members spoke simultaneously and held out their hands.

'One of them was Tuticorin Muthukumaraswami Pillai, the other was Kadayanallur Sankarakrishna Iyer. Both read the letter and touched their eyes with their hands which had held it. Others did the same as they passed the letter around.

'Neelakantha Brahmachari burst into a roar. Every eye turned to him.

'"Friends! Patriot Chidambram Pillai has sent us this message believing we are lion-hearted and true. But a little while ago we behaved like weaklings and womenfolk. All of

148

us wept and sobbed aloud. A professional wake was all that was missing. We can still do it together if you like!"

'His words made everyone feel ashamed.

'"Even you sir, our leader as you are—"

'"Yes, I include myself. I do not blame you alone." The Brahmachari cut in. "We became cowards. True revolutionaries must rejoice at the sufferings of Chidambaram Pillai in prison. Our hearts must turn to stone. Compassion and sympathy must be wiped out. Not only towards our enemies. If we find a traitor among us, we must be ready to chop him to pieces. Only then can we call ourselves the true sons of Mother India!"

'The silence was total. Everyone sat with his head down, not daring to meet the eyes of others. The waves echoed our inner turbulence as they crashed on the shore close by.

'"Friends! We must not drown ourselves in self-recrimination just because we were momentarily overcome. It is good that this happened now. It will help us not to err in the future. Once upon this seashore, two great warriors poured out their devotion to their motherland. Both Chidambaram Pillai and Subramania Siva began their mission here. The flames of that revolution spread fiercely over the whole district. In this very town of Tuticorin, barbers refused to shave those who opposed the Swadeshi movement, washermen refused to launder their clothes. At a word from

149

Chidambaram Pillai, shopkeepers drew the shutters down, labourers refused to work in the mills. Collector Winch came running down to reason with them, beg them, and try every trick in the trade. But Chidambaram Pillai's word was more powerful than the government's orders. This same town and district, where such a brave heart lived, is now frozen in deep slumber . . ."

' "No, if anyone is caught napping, every one in this district is ready to snatch whatever he has in his pocket," said a low voice. I learnt that it belonged to Savadi Arunachalam Pillai.

' "Who spoke? What did he say?" Neelakantha Brahmachari raised his voice menacingly.

'Savadi Pillai answered, "You can wake those who are asleep. But you cannot wake people who pretend to be asleep."

' "No, don't say that. Surely we can rouse them. A single explosion and they will all be with us. Friends! The time for words is over. The time has come for action. How many of you are ready? Raise your hands."

'Everyone put up a hand. I too raised mine. Vanchi Iyer put up both hands.

' "We have been ready for the past six months. It is you who have been saying "Not yet, not yet". Is it possible to assemble the whole nation before we start?" Again Vanchi

Iyer showed impatience. "Vanchi, keep quiet! You think it is impossible to get the whole town to join us. I say it is possible. Revolution will explode in a hundred spots in Tamil Nadu, on the same date and at the same time. On that day, all the white men in the state shall be shot dead, the rule of King George V will come to an end. Immediately after that Chidambaram Pillai shall be crowned King of the Tamils. Every Indian state will witness similar revolutions."

'Some of the group members enquired about the date fixed for the event, others wanted to know what they were to do on that day.

'"I will announce the date and your individual task at the next meeting. Until now we have indulged in mere talk. Therefore we could meet anywhere. But now that the time has come to act, the meeting place, manpower and money must be attuned to action. Friends, I am going to convene our next meeting at Kuttralam on the night of the next full moon. You can find out the details of time and place from our Murugayyan at Kashimajorpuram . . . Murugayya, is it all right with you?"

'That was when I knew for certain who Ponniyamma's husband was.

'"Swami, I am no longer in Kashimajorpuram. I work in Sharma's bungalow at Kuttralam now," Murugayyan said.

'"So much the better, but is Sharma at the bungalow?"

151

'"No sir. Luckily he went off to Tiruvithankur yesterday. It seems he will be away for two months."

'After this, the men dispersed slowly in twos and threes. I left with my hands on the shoulders of Vanchi Iyer and Dharmaraja Iyer. I liked those two immensely.

## 4

'Two weeks passed slowly. Three days before the full moon, Neelakantha Brahmachari planted himself at Ramabhadra Sharma's house. He had a constant stream of visitors. I too went to see him once or twice. Undoubtedly he was a man of learning and keen intelligence. But were things really going to happen the way he said they would? Was the British Empire going to fall in a single day? I was stunned by the very thought. However, I resolved to do my duty.

'When I went to see Neelakantha Brahmachari, I observed that Murugayyan and Ponniyamma led a happy life in their garden hut by the bungalow. Poor things! The Brahmachari had arrived to spoil their joy. I did not fail to note that the lines on Ponniyamma's forehead had increased.

'On the eve of the full moon, the monk came to Sharma's bungalow to offer words of encouragement to Ponniyamma. He opened the gate and entered the compound. There was no one in the garden. The persons who needed information had made their enquiries and gone up the hill. Only

Ponniyamma remained, talking to her five-year-old daughter. When she saw the monk she hurried out of the hut.

'"Swami! Why have you come at this hour? There are no menfolk here!"

'"Ponniyamma, I have not come to spend the night here. I have work up on the mountain tonight. I am leaving at once. I came in such haste only to fulfil my promise to you.'

'"What promise, swami?"

'"About your husband. Have you forgotton it? Or did you think the danger was past?"

'"There's no danger, swami. It is just my woman's mind which became needlessly anxious."

'"Ponniyamma, you are a fool! Someone has deceived you. In fact your husband stands in great danger this very night. The man who was here for the last three days, that Brahmachari rascal, do you know where he has taken your husband? To the Shenbaga Devi temple up the hill. More than twenty persons shall assemble there tonight. They have gathered to sacrifice your husband to the goddess."

'"Ayyo!" Ponniyamma screamed.

'"Well, what did you think? Aren't they sorcerers from Kerala? Still, if you do what I tell you, your husband can be saved."

'"I will, swami!"

'"See, in this letter I have written everything down in

detail. This must be taken to the police station at Tenkasi.
If you do that, the police will stop the sacrifice and save
your husband."

'"Why do you need the police, swami? I will myself go
and save my husband."

'"Silly girl! They are twenty in number. What can you
do against them alone? They will sacrifice you along with
your husband."

'Ponniyamma looked thoughtful.

'"I will go swami," said she as she took the letter.

'"Your husband's death will be on your head if you fail,"
said the swami and walked swiftly away.

'I went up the Kuttralam hills as day swooned into
darkness.

'As I trudged on, lost in thought, I felt I was being
followed. From their voices I guessed there were two persons.
Surely they were Vanchi and Dharmarajan . . . ?

'There was something I had to do before they joined me.
I had planned to wait until it became really dark. But it
could be dangerous if they caught up with me before I did
what I had to do.

'Therefore, as soon as I turned a corner in the mountain
path, I entered the forest, covered a short distance, and hid
myself behind a rock. I took off my disguise. I wrapped the
beard and wig in a big handkerchief and tied it up. I put the

bundle into a tree hollow that I had marked. I returned to the path expecting those two would have gone ahead. But the path was empty as far as the eye could see.

'When I reached the wooden bridge I sensed men coming up behind me. I stopped and waited for them.

'Vanchi and Dharmarajan! However did they manage to elude me on the way? As usual Vanchi had his little leather case. But he carried a small bundle as well.

'The three of us trekked on amidst banter and laughter.

## 5

'It was about ten at night. On the flat rock beside the Shenbaga Devi Falls, some twenty-five men sat in a circle. The place was lit up by crackling logs.

'As before, Neelakantha Brahmachari took the lead.

'He thundered on and on like one possessed. He dwelt on the loss and suffering undergone by the nation since the white man established his rule over the holy land.

'"They destroyed our religion. They destroyed our arts and crafts and industries. They looted all our gold and made off with it. They brought famine to this land of plenitude. Friends! Lord Vishnu, the destroyer of evil and protector of the good, will he let these atrocities go unchecked? Never! To destroy evil and establish righteousness he sent us leaders like Bal Gangadhar Tilak, Bipinchandra Pal and Ashwini Kumar Dutt.

To our beloved land of the Tamils, he sent many, many warriors like Chidambaram Pillai, Subramania Siva and Subramania Bharati. Most of them are in prison now. What of that? Hasn't Bhagwan Krishna himself been an inmate of prison? Did not Prabhu Rama live in the forest? I have been saying that a time will come when the walls of the prison house shall be torn down. Friends, that moment has arrived. NOW!"

'"We are ready!"

'"We are ready!"

'Everyone shrieked aloud. Vanchi Iyer alone murmured, "We have heard all this a hundred times and shouted back responses a hundred times!" Dharmaraja Iyer who was close by told him to stay quiet.

'Neelankantha Brahmachari broke in, "Vanchi is fed up with words, he is eager for action. Fair enough! Let those who have not taken the pledge do so now."

'In the assembled group, twenty men had already taken the pledge. Five had yet to do so. I was one of the five.

'Madathukadai Chidambaram Pillai read out the pledge. The words sounded dreadful.

'"I shall sacrifice my life for the sake of my motherland, for the liberation of Bharat Mata. I shall give implicit obedience to my leader. If I betray my trust, may I be sacrificed to Mother Kali."

'These were the important statements. The pledge had

to be signed in blood—the thumb dipped in the blood from a cut inflicted on your hand and the print affixed on paper. Water reddened with kumkumam had to be drunk before a picture of the Goddess Kali.

'After the ceremony Neelankantha Brahmachari said to us, "Friends, now I can announce the date. It is fixed for the new moon day. All those who have taken the pledge must pick out a white man and keep following him. The job must be finished on new moon day. After that, try to escape. If you can't escape shoot yourselves and enter the warriors' heaven! Those who don't possess arms may go to Puducheri and take what they need. But we are short of funds. Therefore, before the new moon, all of you must collect at least a thousand rupees and hand it over to me."

'Vanchi Iyer stood up. Looking straight at our chief he asked, "Sir, what is the truth behind the newspaper reports?"

'"What news? Which report?" the Brahmachari thundered.

'"The bulletin issued by the Aurobindo Ghosh Ashram mentions you by name and says that you have no connection whatsoever with the ashram. I am asking you if this is true."

'The Brahmachari burst into fearful laughter. "What are you saying? Do you doubt your own leader? What kind of declaration do you expect from the Aurobindo Ghosh Ashram? To accept responsibility for my actions? If they do, can they continue to function in Puducheri? And carry on with their work? Fool! Doesn't this elementary truth strike your thick head? Tomorrow, if the police arrest you, and question you, will you write down all our names for them?"

'Vanchi replied calmly, "Sir, I don't need to write our names down for the police. With one or two exceptions, the Tenkasi police station has all our names. So my nephew in Tenkasi informed me this evening. He is a clerk at the police station. It seems an anonymous letter has reached the police. He warned me to be careful."

'"Then there is a traitor in this group. Who is he? In the name of Mother Kali, let him own up!"

'"There . . . ! There's Mother Kali!" bellowed Subbiah Pillai. We turned to where be pointed. At a little distance, on the edge of a rock, a woman stood with flying hair and tearful eyes. She was breathing hard. It was possible to mistake her for Mother Kali. However, I could see that she was no avenging goddess, but Ponniyamma.

'Murugayyan knew so too. He looked at our chief.

'"Sir, the woman is my wife Ponni. Let me find out why she is here."

'As soon as Murugayyan walked away, Vanchi said, "Don't you understand what I told you? Someone has come to know of our secret meeting. That woman had a letter with her this evening. It was addressed to the Tenkasi police station.

It contained information about our meeting here."

'"How do you know all this?" Sankara Iyer's anger rang out.

'Murugayyan and Ponniyamma came up to the group. She had a letter in her hand. Murugayyan handed it over to the chief.

'Running his eyes over it the chief asked, "This is a strange letter. Who gave it to you, Amma?"

'"A bearded monk gave it to me, sir!" Ponniyamma answered. "I have often seen him here at Shenbaga Devi."

'"Can anyone guess the informer's identity?"

'"Who is it? If you know his name, say it without fear."

'"There . . . ! That man looks flustered. Ask him to open his bundle."

'"Subbiah Pillai, take Vanchi's bundle and see what it contains."

'Subbiah Pillai pounced upon Vanchi, grabbed his bundle and opened it. Out fell a wig and a beard.

'"Friends! There is no doubt that Vanchinathan is the traitor. And this letter is in his handwriting!" Neelakantha Brahmachari shrieked.

'Meanwhile, Vanchi did not remain idle. Before anyone could guess what he was up to, he had opened his leather case and jumped up with a shining revolver in his hand.

'Vanchi swung the revolver around to point it successively

at every one of us and said, "Friends! This revolver has six bullets. I had reserved them for an important task—to take revenge on those who had forced Chidambaram Pillai to work in the oil mill. I have kept them to reward Collector Ashe. But if anyone tries to close in, don't blame me for the consequences. Again I warn you, I am not the traitor here, though I have an idea who he is. Run for your lives. If you save yourselves now, you may be able to fulfil your vows later. As for you, oh great chief Erukoor Neelakantha Brahmachari! Go back to the village, get married, and live snugly ever after! You cannot mastermind a revolution. Your rebellion is confined to words alone . . . Murugayya, ask your wife, she may perhaps be able to tell you more about the informer!"

'With this volcanic explosion, Vanchi Iyer sprinted away. Dharmaraja Iyer raced to catch up with him.

'For a moment the others stood transfixed. Then they too scattered in all directions. Only Murugayyan, Ponniyamma and I remained.

'"Sir, all the madmen have run away. Are you going home with us, or will you stay here to meditate on Shenbaga Devi?" Murugayyan asked me.

'"I am coming with you," I replied.

'We took the short cut by the falls. We reached the top of the hill from where the Periya Aruvi (Big Falls) begins.

'"My goodness! How will you feel if you tumble down

from here?" Murugayyan wondered aloud. To which Ponniyamma retorted, "What a question to ask!"

'We were half-way down and at the pool named Pongumangadal.

'With its ever-spilling waters, the pool made a lovely sight in the moonlight. Even though the waterfall was not in full spate, the pool overflowed tempestuously.

'"My God! What is this?"

'In a split second I found myself in the swirling pool.

'As soon as I reached the bank Murugayyan stretched his hand out to me. But why are they pushing me back instead of hauling me out?

'Husband and wife, why do they laugh? Has the full moon driven them mad?

'My arms and legs were worn out to exhaustion when the blessed couple dragged me out and left me half-dead on the bank. I had gone under a couple of times and thought my life was over. But at least they let me live! For this act of kindness, may their family thrive for many generations to come.'

## 6

The old man with hair as white as the tumbai flower stopped his tale at this point. But I knew the story was not over.

'What happened after that?' I asked.

'After that? Well, it is public knowledge now. The very next day at Maniyachi Junction, Vanchi Iyer shot Collector Ashe dead, and shot again to kill himself. Fourteen men, including Neelakantha Brahmachari, were charged with sedition and punished for it too.'

'Surely Murugayyan was not one of them.'

'No, because his name did not figure in the list leaked to the police. He was lucky. Ponni was also lucky.'

'That's all right. But why did Ponni and Murugayyan push you into the pool? Why did they torture you?'

'The fools thought I was the traitor, that it was I who informed the police. That is why they punished me.'

'Blockheads! That is why I think it is necessary to be educated.'

'Yes, that is why we say education is important. But most surprisingly, those illiterate fools managed somehow to guess the truth.'

'What! Then . . . it was you!'

'Why else should I be wandering through all these years without a moment's peace?'

'But the letters? Vanchi Iyer's handwriting . . . ?'

'Oh great teller of tales! Haven't you guessed it yet? What kind of stories do you write anyway? Hadn't I been sentenced to seven years for forgery? I forged Chidambaram Pillai's hand. I also forged Vanchi's Iyer's writing. Do you ask me

162

why? Why do you write stories? Isn't it natural for anyone to engage himself in whatever he is fond of doing? Besides, I did have some hopes of a reward from the British sarkar . . .'

As he spoke we heard the tinkling laughter of children. Five or six children, a young man and woman, a grandfather and a grandmother, were all coming past the Shenbaga Devi temple towards us.

I looked behind me. The old man was not there. He had vanished like magic. His wig and beard bobbed in the waters below.

The old lady came up to me and asked, 'Why sir, wasn't there another man with you?'

'No Amma, I was alone,' I lied. I then asked her, 'What is your name, Grandma?'

'Ponniyamma.'

'The old man's name?'

'How can I say it? It is another name for Lord Subrahmanya.'

'Murugayyan?'

'Yes!'

'Are they your grandchildren?'

'Yes sir! Do pray to the goddess for the children's welfare.'

'I will,' I said.

For about half an hour I stood under the waterfall and then began to go downhill.

163

I blessed the Mahatma who obtained freedom for India through ahimsa, without any of the horrors of violence. Isn't that the reason why the children of this Tamil land are able to laugh and play so happily today?

# THE S. S. MENAKA

'S.S. Menaka'
*Kalki* (1942)

*T*he S. S. Menaka was on the high seas. The ship had never been thus overloaded before, and this load consisted mostly of passengers. Like bees around the hive, passengers swarmed all over the ship, leaving not even an inch of space free.

The first and the second classes had only White passengers, largely women and children. The Blacks who occupied the rest of the ship were a mixed group of Hindus and Muslims. They spoke many languages—Tamil, Bengali, Malayalam, Punjabi and Sinhalese. There were men and women of all ages. They had neither place to sleep nor the facilities to bathe. It was many days since they had washed themselves; it would have been difficult to find a filthier group of people. Each sat in a morose stupor, with a trunk or bundle by his side. Their grief, terror and dejection were indescribable. Some of them were dazed by the atrocities they had witnessed. Others appeared to have spent their nights at a horror show. A few seemed afflicted by a fatal curse. They had all gone through the ordeal of starvation.

Huge crowds are invariably marked by din. But on this ship people hardly spoke to one another. When someone did speak his voice rang hollow, as if it came out of a deep well. The weak, intermittent cries of children were heartrending.

The ship was an eyesore, covered with trash and garbage. Cleanliness and order were things unknown. The stench was

167

unbearable. What a variety of bad odours! The smells of fresh paint, onions rotting in the corners, stale bread, human sweat, cheroot smoke, children making a mess everywhere . . . was this hell?

There is no need to explain in detail the reasons for the conditions prevalent on board. It is enough to say that the ship sailed from Singapore in early February 1942, a few days before the Japanese attack on the city. After six days of travel, the passengers remained ignorant of their location at sea. No one was certain of their ultimate destination. The ship was believed to be heading towards Colombo. But only God knew when and if it would reach that port. The passengers were traumatized more by mental agony than by the physical discomforts they endured on the voyage. Many of them had seen the devastation caused by Japanese bombs dropped in Malaya. They would never forget those horrors as long as they lived. If the Japanese bombs could cause such havoc on land, what would happen if a bomb fell upon the ship in mid-ocean? Total annihilation! The passengers found themselves constantly scanning the skies.

But was the danger confined to the skies alone? It could come floating on the waves. It could erupt suddenly from under the sea. For quite some time now there had been rumours of Japan's warships and submarines nosing through the Indian Ocean and the Bay of Bengal. No one

168

really believed he would live to reach home. Under the circumstances, how could any passenger be bright and lively?

And yet, among the thousand passengers on board, there was a woman whose face remained bright. Whenever it showed signs of fading away, the woman drew her brightness out of a box by her side and applied it to her face! Her eyes were lightly lined in black. There was a red dot on her forehead. Her hair was plaited neatly. Three or four times a day she managed to procure clean water to wash her face and touch it up with powder and make-up. She lacked nothing but a string of fresh flowers for her hair. But she had pinned a colourful artificial bloom in its place. When she walked up and down, a mild jasmine scent came wafting through the pervasive stench.

It was not surprising that the woman should have aroused disgust in the other passengers. Their faces reflected this revulsion whenever they happened to look at her. Many pointed to her and exchanged whispers. A few spoke loudly enough for her to overhear—'Devil!' 'Slut!' 'Why did the bitch have to board this ship?' 'Will she powder herself even at the moment of death?' 'Does she think she can cast her spell on the god of death?'

Their talk revealed that the woman's name was Rajani. She had pursued a notorious career in Singapore. 'Miss Rajani' was painted on her trunk. It was impossible to guess

169

her age. She seemed very young; if she did sometimes appear older, it was owing to the life of dissipation she had led. At other times she seemed an older woman whose youthful looks came from her heavy use of cosmetics.

Who could help feeling repulsed by a woman like her? A woman who behaved as she did when death stared them in the face, at a time when there was no guarantee of life beyond the present moment!

Yet there was someone on the ship who did not find her repulsive. In fact he showed more concern than was seemly. Such behaviour would have been surprising even in a passenger, but he was an officer, the ship's assistant engineer. He looked like an Anglo-Indian, yet he spoke chaste Tamil. His colleagues called him John.

Assistant engineer John came to the top deck at least twice a day. Rajani would get up and join him. They stood leaning against the rails. They didn't talk much. Mostly they gazed at the sky. Sometimes very furtively John brought her a slice of bread. It was extremely difficult to come by food on board, but Rajani had to be coaxed to accept it.

The other passengers did not relish these meetings. 'See, even on the ship she has trapped someone,' they said and talked of lodging a complaint against her with the captain.

That evening Rajani told John, 'The passengers resent our talking to each other.'

170

'Do we? I hadn't heard our voices until just now!'

Rajani laughed aloud. It struck a discordant note in the miasma of fear and despair which shrouded the ship.

Becoming aware of it herself, Rajani looked quickly around and added, 'They cannot bear to see us together, even for a little while. They want to complain to the captain.'

'Why are they so angry with you?'

'I wish I knew. Was it I who snatched their freedom and possessions away? What is the use of making me the target of the rage which should be directed at the Japanese? They are stupid. They don't like me washing my face and putting a pottu on it. We may die any moment now. Why can't we try to appear pleasant as long as we stay alive? What do we gain by remaining unwashed and unkempt?'

'Why do you harp on death all the time? Do you want to die?'

Rajani answered with a single word, 'Yes.'

'Why?'

'What is the use of staying alive?'

'Don't you have friends and relatives in India?'

'No.'

'If you really want to die, there is no time like tonight. The moon rises at nine o'clock. After that the sea will seem like an ocean of milk.'

'I'm ready,' said Rajani.

171

That evening her fellow-travellers were astonished and repelled to see Rajani getting dressed at sunset. They did not hesitate to display their disgust.

Rajani was not bothered by their reaction. She was lost in a deep reverie. Her excitement mounted with each hour.

The ship sailed much faster than usual, as if in response to her mental state. Her fellow-travellers discussed this increase of speed with anxiety.

When John came to the top deck at about eight o'clock, Rajani hastened to his side.

'Ready? No doubts in your mind?'

'None.'

'Then come with me,' said John and walked ahead. Since it was wartime, the lights were out; there was total darkness.

John's white uniform helped Rajani to follow him in the dark.

Once when she stumbled, John turned back and caught her by the hand. Rajani felt a deep thrill. Both walked on in silence.

'Careful! There are steps here,' said John.

They climbed down.

After fifteen minutes John stopped walking. There was the sound of a door being opened. A sharp cold breeze entered and hit Rajani on the face with the spray from the waves.

172

'I'm asking you for the last time. You don't have any doubts about this, do you?' said John.

'Not at all.'

'We have to go down a ladder hanging outside this door. The boat will rock hard. Don't be afraid. Hold me tight.'

'Such careful and elaborate preparations for death!' said Rajani. And yet she held John's hand tightly.

They climbed down.

The boat was buffeted strongly by the swell rising from the side of the ship.

Holding Rajani's hand in his strong grip, John unhooked the chain which held the boat to the ship.

As soon as it was adrift, the boat rocked alarmingly from side to side. It was a lifeboat and it did not capsize.

In the dim light of the stars it could be seen that within a matter of minutes, a great distance separated boat and ship.

'Ayyo! How will you return to the ship?'

'What's this! Didn't I warn you well in advance?'

'I'm not worried for myself. Shouldn't you go back?'

'Why should I go back?'

'It is I who have lost interest in life.'

'So have I.'

'But you have your work on board. Who will do it now?'

'I have no work tonight. There will be no necessity for anyone to work tomorrow.'

173

'What are you saying?'

'Wait for half an hour and you'll know.'

After a pause Rajani asked, 'Did you also come away to die?'

'No. I came away to keep myself alive. For a few hours more.'

'I don't understand.'

'If you must know, I'll tell you. A Japanese submarine has sighted the S. S. Menaka and is pursuing the ship now. The people on board have just half an hour more to live.'

'Ayyo!'

'We can keep ourselves alive for a few hours longer.'

'Why?'

'Why should we die? We should try our best to preserve the life God has given us.'

At that moment a brilliant flash made Rajani turn to look back. A sudden conflagration in the middle of the black ocean made a fearful spectacle. At the same instant there was a horrendous explosion, like the simultaneous burst of a thousand bolts of thunder.

Rajani had heard bombs exploding in Malaya. But they had been nothing like this stupendous crash. Rajani thought her head had split into a thousand fragments.

John held her tight and said, 'Don't be afraid!'

When Rajani, shell-shocked, opened her eyes again, she

174

saw thick huge clouds of black smoke swirling up from the spot where the fire had blazed before.

'The ship has sunk,' said John.

'Ayyo! With all those people! Such brutality! So many children. Are the Japanese human beings or demons?'

Monstrous waves rose from the sinking ship and assaulted the boat. Rajani was amazed to see the boat still afloat despite their tremendous force.

In a little while the black smoke clouds spread everywhere and blanketed the sky and sea in total darkness. Rajani had never seen such macabre darkness before.

She gripped John's shoulders with all the strength left in her trembling hands.

After some time the darkness began to lift. Once again stars twinkled in the sky.

'Why ever did you bring me away! By now, along with the other passengers, I too would have—'

'Look!' John exclaimed.

There was a golden glow on the horizon.

'What's that! My God! Not another ship!'

'No, no. It is the moon rising in the east.'

Even as they were looking, the moon rose as if fresh from a bath in the sea. Where the sky met the sea, the waters shone like molten gold.

'How . . . how splendid!'

175

'I knew it would be splendid. I brought you so that we could watch this splendour together and die.'

'Why talk of death? We can try to be happy as long as we are alive.'

'That's exactly what I was going to say to you.'

'How can we be happy? Ayyo! Every one of those passengers is dead now. How the children would have suffered!'

'Look at you! And after saying you wanted to talk about pleasant things!'

'Any pleasant things left to talk about?'

'We can talk about the happy times in our lives.'

'You can begin,' said Rajani.

'Nowadays it is customary to give women the lead in everything.'

'In the course of my entire life, I have tasted happiness only for a single month. But recollections of that month have tormented me ever since.'

'Don't talk about the torment now, only the happy times.'

'I will start to weep if I talk about it.'

'Try and see if you can make it into a story.'

After a short pause, Rajani began to speak.

'Twenty years ago, a young girl lived with her father and mother in a little house in Royapuram. At one time they had been wealthy. The father had lost all his property in his business ventures. The experience had unsettled his mind.

'He began to attend the races, hoping to recover his losses through gambling. In the process even the few remaining family jewels were snatched away. The entreaties of mother and daughter fell on deaf ears.

'They hung a board saying "To Let" outside their house hoping to rent out the small room they had upstairs. A young man became their tenant. He worked at the harbour. Father liked him very much. A few days after he moved in, father told the young man he should not ruin his health by eating out. He could have his meals in the house. The young man agreed.

'The poor girl thought that it was for her sake that the young man had accepted the arrangement. Until a year earlier she had been studying in a convent school. She had stuffed her head with every novel she could get and lived in a world of romance and fantasy. She believed it was love at first sight with them. The young man confirmed her faith. He hunted for opportunities to meet her alone.

'"Meeting you has made a new man of me," he often told her. He added, "I have never been so happy before." The girl thought she had attained celestial bliss. But she was too shy to speak. She listened to him in silence.

'One day he said to her, "I chatter all the time. But you never open your mouth." When she did not speak even after that, he said, "At least answer me this. Shall I stay or go away from this house?"

"'Stay," said the girl. He at once seized her hand boldly and said, "Thank you very much." The look on his face at that moment seemed to say, "I am ready to sacrifice my whole life for you."

Rajani fell silent.

'Then?' asked John.

'That very same person did go away because he didn't have the heart to "sacrifice" twenty rupees.'

'Did he refuse to part with twenty rupees when she asked him for it?'

'No, no. The girl would rather have killed herself than ask him for money,' Rajani continued. 'When those two were lost in a world of daydreams, one day the father asked the girl for the key to her steel trunk. He had lost the key to his desk and wished to see if her key could unlock it. The girl gave him the key.

'The next day the tenant asked if the maidservant was given to stealing. Ten rupees were missing from his trunk. The girl asked him if he kept his trunk locked. He replied that though he did keep it locked, it was no great matter to find a duplicate key to fit the lock. The girl's mind flew to her father. She remembered that the horse races had been held the previous day. She was disconcerted. Her face must

178

have revealed her agitation. She did not know if he noted her change of expression or what he thought about it. The young man left for work without further comment.

'That afternoon the girl asked her father to return her key. "I have lost it somewhere," he replied. "But you do have a duplicate, don't you?"

'The girl's suspicions increased. For the next five or six days, she went through all the tortures of hell. She tried her best to hide her feelings. The young man did not appear to have noticed anything amiss with her. Nor did he again refer to the loss of money.

'The races were held again on Saturday. The girl kept a close watch on her father from the morning. As usual the man upstairs left for the harbour at 8 a.m. A little later she saw her father going up the stairs. She followed him stealthily. What was he going to do? It was exactly as she had feared. He unlocked the trunk in the room upstairs and removed two ten-rupee notes from it. The girl felt a thunderbolt crashing over her. She ran away before her father could see her. She spent a long time thinking about the problem.

'She knew that nothing short of murder would result if she raised the issue at that time. She knew the monstrous lure of gambling. So she waited impatiently for her father to finish eating and leave the house.

'During her schooldays, the girl had saved thirty rupees

without her father's knowledge. She took twenty rupees from her savings, and the duplicate key to her own trunk and went up again.

'With trembling hands she unlocked the trunk and was about to replace the money when a sudden sound made her turn back. On the staircase she saw the top of a head. She heard hurried footsteps going down the stairs. For five whole minutes she sat as if she had turned to stone. Her limbs had become lifeless. When she pulled herself together and went downstairs, she did not see him. He never came back.

'Two days later there was a letter from him. It said urgent work had recalled him to his home town. He might not return. He hoped his belongings and the money in his trunk would cover the cost of his board and lodging.'

'Was the girl terribly upset over his sudden disappearance?' John asked.

'Yes. She was upset. She shed incessant tears. She nearly went mad. Her sorrow was greatly increased by the thought that he had left with the impression that she was nothing but a common thief,' Rajani answered him.

'What did she do after that?' John's voice was husky with emotion.

'After that her life had nothing but horror and misery. I don't want to talk about it. Please don't ask me any more.'

'No, I won't,' answered John.

'It is your turn now,' said Rajani.

'Shall I complete your story?'

'Please do.'

'All right, listen. When the young man saw the girl before the open trunk in the room upstairs, he felt his head would split into fragments. Not satisfied with stealing his heart, the girl was trying to steal his money as well! The girl, to whom he wished to offer his body, soul and all his worldly goods, had unlocked his trunk with a duplicate key to steal petty cash! Her sidelong glances and assurances of love were nothing but pretence and deceit! She was a fraud! Maddened by this thought, the man ran away as fast as he could. He vowed never to return. He cursed all women. Then he cursed himself for having been such easy prey.

'But as time went by his thoughts took another direction. His anger cooled down. He grew calm. He wondered if the girl's action was so reprehensible after all. Extreme poverty had prompted her action. She must have done it for her parents.

'With such thoughts his love grew stronger and he came back in search of the girl. But strangers occupied the house now. They knew nothing about the family which had lived there before them. No one in the neighbourhood had any information to give him. The young man became bitter. Hoping to get over his grief, he converted to Christianity. But

181

this brought him no peace of mind. Since he could not remain in the same place, he gave up his job in the harbour and became a member of a ship's crew. What a fortunate decision it turned out to be! Otherwise, would he have met his beloved Rajam after the passage of twenty years, on the high seas?'

'How did you know the woman you saw on board was the unfortunate Rajammal?' Rajani asked him.

'How did I know? With every nerve in my body I knew it was Rajam. Besides, she has not changed all that much! She appears just as she did when I saw her twenty years ago. But how did Rajam recognize me? I have changed completely.'

'So what if you look different? You can deceive the eyes, but can you deceive the heart? Besides, I had a burning wish to see this man at least once before I died. I wanted him to know I was no petty thief. I was convinced that the opportunity would be granted to me. Something told me this sea voyage was my last journey. In that case, I had to meet him on the ship. When I heard the name "John", my heart told me it was the same Janakiraman who had abandoned me twenty years ago.'

The moon had travelled part way up the heavenly dome. The level waters of the calm sea reflected his silvery form so clearly as to create the illusion of a rival moon on the ocean.

The boat moved gently towards the direction where the moon had risen.

'Do you remember we sang together one day, sitting on the seashore in Royapuram, with the moon shining as gloriously as it is now?' Janakiraman asked.

'Of course,' replied Rajammal.

'Shall we sing again today?'

'Yes!'

And under the enchanting glow of the young moon, in the middle of the tranquil ocean, a deep male voice and a sweet feminine voice rose together in joyful song.

# THE RUINED FORT

'Idinda Kottai'
*Ananda Vikatan* (1940)

*R*ecently, when I visited an old friend, his daughter asked me, 'Uncle, why have you stopped writing stories?' I gave her many excuses. The war had made paper scarce; how could I accommodate the stories of other writers in *The Vikatan* if I kept on writing, so on and so forth. I will now tell you the real reason why I stopped writing.

The more I watch real life events, the more I lose interest in fiction. So many amazing things happen in life, which are beyond the fantasies of fiction. No one doubts their veracity, no one wonders if such things can take place. A report in print is enough to establish the credibility of such events, even if they occur in faraway places.

Take this bizarre episode from last month. After their wedding in Bangalore, a poor couple were walking on the highway, along with the rest of the marriage party, when the bride stopped under a tree for a brief rest. Just then, a branch broke and it crashed over her head. She died on the spot.

This accident was reported in the papers. Would we have believed it if it had occurred in fiction? We would have raised a thousand objections. 'Why did the bride chose to rest under that very tree? Why not some other tree? Couldn't that branch have crashed five minutes before it did? Could it not have fallen on someone else's head?'

When I think of all this, I wonder why I should write fiction at all. If I indeed have to write something

187

to satisfy people like my friend's daughter, why not write about a true incident taken from life? That's what I plan to do now.

Some seven or eight years ago, I made a trip to Tiruvannamalai with two of my friends. We intended to see the Lord of Annamalai, Sage Ramana and S.V.V. At that time, S.V.V wrote frequently about a sophisticated lady called Jaya. We were eager to meet the fortunate man who had such a won-derful helpmeet in life.

The Chenji Fort is situated en route from Madras to Tiruvannamalai. I had long been eager to see it. On the way, we stopped near the fort and explored the historical spot. The more we viewed the ruins of palaces, antahpurams, mandapams, walls, granaries and stables, the more our excitement at the start of the journey gave way to depression. And yet, those structures held a strange attraction of their own. We left the place half-heartedly after wandering among the ruins for a long time.

It was night by the time we reached Tiruvannamalai. Without an instant's delay, we hastened to S.V.V's house and woke him up to ask if he was indeed the man we had come to see. 'And how is Jaya? How are her false teeth?' were the kind of queries with which we satisfied ourselves.

The next day we also obtained the darshan of the Lord

of Annamalai and Sage Ramana. We started for Madras in the evening when the heat of the day lessened.

The car reached Chenji at sunset. I wanted to get down there for a second look. My friends refused to join me. 'You go if you like. We'll go and try to get a cup of coffee,' they said. They expected the very mention of coffee to make me drop the idea of getting down. But the longing in my heart was greater than the lure of coffee.

'I have to see it again,' said I and got down. 'We will return in half an hour. You must be ready to leave by then,' my friends said and drove away in a burst of noise.

When the car had left, the lonely spot was filled with such a silence that I was startled by the sound of my own footsteps. I felt a tingling disquietude as I walked through that empty stretch. But I tried to banish my fears by telling myself that they were irrational.

The sun suddenly dropped behind the hillocks in the west. Darkness came swiftly. I passed old, ruined monuments. I could hear the fluttering wings of bats inside the dark chambers. My fears increased. Fortunately the full moon rose in the east. The moonlight became brighter every minute. I would have certainly turned back if there had not been a full moon.

There are steps cut into the hill behind the ruins. Midway up the steps you get an overview of the landscape round the ruined fort. It was for this view that I had ventured so far. I began to climb the steps. When I reached the bend after the thirtieth step, I froze in astonishment. A man sat there. He was young, well-dressed in veshti and kurta, his hair smartly styled, and he looked intelligent. Coming across such a person anywhere else would not have aroused fear or surprise. But seeing him at that time, and in that deserted place, affected me as if I had stepped on a snake.

The man too looked surprised and bemused. It was he who first pulled himself together. 'Who are you, sir?' he asked. 'You seem to be a stranger in these parts.'

Heartened by the sound of his voice, I felt glad to have found a companion for the return trip. I told him why I had come to that spot.

'I come here quite often,' he said. 'I too love to see this scene in the moonlight.'

Sitting next to him I asked, 'Are you from around this place?'

'No,' he replied. 'I am from Periyakulam. For the last four years, I have been teaching in a school in the village close by.'

His name was Kumaraswami, he had finished his training as a secondary school teacher and had now to fend for himself. His parents were dead.

'Are you not married?' I asked.

190

'Marriage?' he exclaimed and looked up at the moon. 'Not yet,' he sighed with a strange look in his eyes and a half-smile. Then he added, 'But I am engaged.'

'Who is the girl?'

'She is from this region, this very place. It is three hundred years since we became engaged . . .' He paused hesitantly before announcing, 'We are going to be married today.'

My heart began to beat fast. Ayyo! He must surely be mad! And I am trapped here in this lonely spot after sunset!

As I tried to get up and leave unnoticed, he said as if he had read my mind, 'You think I am insane. That is but natural. Sometimes I too wonder if all this is nothing but delusion. If you have time to spare, I will tell you about it. For a long time I have yearned to share my experiences with another person.'

I no longer thought he was mad. I felt that he had undergone deep sorrows, and that those overwhelming sorrows made him speak in the way he did.

'I will listen if you keep it short,' I said.

Kumaraswami looked at me with grateful eyes. 'I promise to be brief,' said he and began his story with a big sigh.

'Didn't I tell you that it is four years since I became a teacher in the next village? Six months after coming here, I visited this Chenji Fort with friends. Somehow this deserted place captivated my heart. I wanted to return here again and again. Whenever I managed to get company, I did just that. After a while, it became difficult to get anyone to come with me. Everyone I knew refused saying, "What's there in that graveyard?" Then I started coming here with some of my students. In time they too got tired of these visits.

'Then I began to come alone. I would come on Sundays and holidays, wander round and round the ruins and return before dark.

'Once, about a year ago, I happened to come here on a full moon night. Like today, the round moon rained silver. Reluctant to leave, I began to weave fantasies . . . Three hundred years ago, this place would have been full of life. The gates of the fort would be clanged shut in the distance; auspicious musical instruments would be playing in the palace; soldiers on horseback riding up and down; temple bells ringing for the evening service; lovely women dancing in the theatres; princesses walking in the palace with tinkling anklets . . .

'Suddenly, in the midst of this reverie, I felt my hair stand on end. What was that! I seemed to hear the sound of real anklets! I listened closely, with rapt attention. I seemed to hear the distant tinkle of a woman's anklets as she came walking. Did that sound belong to this world or to some other world? Was it a memory from some previous birth? I also felt that sometime, somewhere, I had heard it before.

'My whole body was drenched with sweat. I stood up and shook myself hard in order to free myself from that illusion. I rushed home. I didn't sleep a wink that night. Those who saw me the next morning said, "Why, you look pale, as if you've seen a ghost!" Who could say whether I had indeed returned from the realm of ghosts the previous night? I resolved never to step into this fort again. But that resolution weakened with the passage of time. As the time for the next full moon approached, a desire rose in me to come here again. Finally, on the day itself, I was unable to withstand the pull. I felt that some awesome power drew me here.

'I came and sat right where we are sitting now. The moon was floating up like a gold disc. It was about two or three hours after sundown. I rose to leave, thinking that the anklets I had heard before were merely an illusion. I had hardly got up when once again the sweet anklets began to tinkle. At first they seemed to come from a great distance, from another world. With every second, they came nearer. After that, I could not stay on. I began to run, slowing down only when I was certain that the anklets were not following me. And yet, I did not stop shivering until I reached home.

'I gave up all notions of avoiding this place. I began to

193

come whenever I found time. I was disappointed when my frequent visits brought no repetition of that experience. The feeling that the sound of the anklets may somehow be connected to the full moon made me come back on the next full moon night. That was when my suspicions were confirmed. The anklets tinkled as before. This time I did not leave. I sat back, determined to witness the events unfold. The anklets came nearer and nearer. They stopped when they reached the step right here before us. A rare fragrance seemed to accompany the sound, a subtle scent of sandalwood. Was it really a scent? Or only the memory of some scent? I couldn't say.

'I froze like a statue. I was in a state of trance. The tinkling began again. I felt it rise over the steps and stop just behind me. The soft perfume of sandalwood surrounded me. I felt it with every pore of my body. I don't know for how long I was lost in a daze. Then, just over my head, I heard a heart-rending sob. Drops of water fell on me. I got up, and was startled out of my wits when a silken cloth brushed past me. Too scared to linger after that, I raced down the steps, trembling all over.

'I waited eagerly for the next full moon day, cursing myself for running home the last time. The day came at long last and found me as usual on this very step here. It seemed as if the anklets moved very hesitantly that day. They stopped before me and then went on to stand behind me. The sweet scent of sandalwood enveloped me with no uncertain power. I felt two blossom-like arms encircle my shoulders. A thrill shot through me from head to foot. Since the sensation seemed so real, I raised my arms to touch the hands that embraced me. But in vain. I looked back in dismay. All I saw was empty space. I must have swooned. The moon was high up in the sky by the time I recovered consciousness. Somehow, I managed to stumble home. I experienced goose-pimples everytime I recalled that embrace which immersed me in such joyful rapture and made me faint.

'When the sun rose on the morrow, I thought the previous evening's experience had been mere hallucination. I was afraid that I was suffering from a madness which increased day by day. I vowed not to go anywhere near the fort again. But my fear that it was all an illusion was shattered very soon. Some of my students asked me, "Sir, did you go to a wedding? There's a strong smell of sandalwood coming from you!"

'So, my experience was no delusion. It was true that a fascinating enchantress was pursuing me every full moon night. Who was she? Why did she come in search of a poor schoolmaster? Would I ever see her form? Would I ever know the secret of this extraordinary experience?

'I had my answer on the next full moon night. As usual,

when I heard the anklets, I turned to look in the direction from which they came. I was thrilled and astounded to see the form of a woman coming towards me. She didn't seem to be walking, rather she was floating along. Was she real or unreal? As she came nearer and nearer, I became certain that it was indeed a real woman.

'She wore a skirt and davani like the Rajput women I had seen in pictures. Her jewels were in the same style. The end of her davani was draped over her head. When the moon fell on her face, it seemed as if her face was the source of that light.

'Her face seemed familiar. Sometime, somewhere, I had seen that woman, talked and sported with her. But where? When? As I pondered over this mystery, she came to stand beside me and looked at me with her wide eyes. Her tears sparkled like pearls in the moonlight. "Kumar! Do you remember me?" she asked. When that sweet voice fell on my ears, I felt my heart would burst. As if in a dream of long ago, I recalled having held her hand and sworn never to forget her, not only in this life, but in all my subsequent births as well. I fainted before I could reply.'

I don't know if Kumaraswami's tale sounds credible to you as you read this, but it sounded utterly convincing when he narrated it. The ambience of that place and time must have cast their spell on me. Kumaraswami stopped at this point, and got up to take a keen look around.

'And what happened after that?' I asked eagerly.

Kumaraswami continued his story.

'When I recovered consciousness, I found my head on this woman's lap, and felt her soft hands stroking my forehead. I leapt up and sat down at a little distance from her.

'"Kumar! Why are you afraid? Don't you remember me? I am your Malati." Her words sounded like a melody.

'Malati! Malati! What a sweet name! I repeated it several times in my heart.

'"Try to remember, Kumar! Once long ago, didn't you leave me at this very spot, on just such a night, when the full moon spread its milky radiance? I urged you not to forget me. You swore with your hand on mine that you would never forget, not only in that life but in every subsequent birth. Don't you remember?" Malati asked.

'Didn't I tell you that this very scene had flashed in my mind rather hazily before I lost consciousness? I was now certain that it was no delusion, but a real-life experience.

'I looked at Malati. She was gazing at me with boundless love. I saw tears standing in her wide eyes. I was moved. I held her hands and replied, "Yes, Malati, I do remember. Again I swear to you that I will remember you in all my births."

197

'By slow degrees, she reminded me of our previous history. As she talked, I could recall, as in old dreams, the experiences of three hundred years ago.'

Kumaraswami paused here to ask if I knew anything of the history of the Chenji Fort. I replied that I knew of Raja Tej Singh's association with it, but nothing more.

'The tale of Raja Tej Singh is only a legend. There is no evidence for its veracity. But I am going to tell you of a true incident. Some three hundred years ago, Raja Prithvi Singh ruled at Chenji. He belonged to a valiant Rajput clan. It seems an ancestor of his came down south and built this fort for himself as he didn't want to be a vassal to the Pathans in Delhi. His descendants became independent chieftains ruling over this fort and the surrounding region. Despite repeated attempts, the Mughal forces could not capture this fort. Prithvi Singh remained the free ruler of this small kingdom.

'The king had a daughter called Malati. Her tutor had a son named Sukumaran. As children, they had studied together. Sukumaran had a deep interest in music. When he grew up he went on a long journey to acquire proficiency in the art. For a while he learnt Carnatic music at Tanjavur and Vijayanagaram. Then he went to Maharashtra to learn abhangs, which were then becoming popular. From there he travelled to Delhi to learn Hindustani music from the disciples of Tansen.

198

'Upon his return, he held a concert in the royal court. Malati heard her childhood playmate's music from a curtained balcony. Perhaps because he knew this, Sukumaran surpassed himself that day. His singing did not seem to belong to the earth. He poured forth the music of the celestial bards. The whole court was enchanted. Princess Malati's enjoyment exceeded that of all others. She offered her heart as the reward for the joy she felt.

'Some time later, Malati told her father that she wanted to learn music from Sukumaran. Though women remained strictly behind the veil in those days, the king yielded to his daughter's request because Sukumaran was the son of her old tutor.

'As she belonged to a northern clan, Malati was naturally drawn to Hindustani music in which she began to take lessons from Sukumaran. Love grew between them. Sukumaran warned her several times that their love was bound to end in disaster. But Malati would not listen. She kept insisting that she would marry him; she would somehow manage to win her father's consent to it. But a sudden danger came to threaten not only their love, but the whole kingdom as well. The Nawabs of Arcot had long regarded the Rajas of Chenji as their allies. They had taken assistance from the Chenji kings in their battles with the Mughal forces from the north. They did not extract any tribute from Chenji.

'Hearing of the beauty of Princess Malati, the then Nawab of Arcot—who had heard of marriages between the Badshahs of Delhi and Rajput maidens— decided he would follow their example and marry a Rajput woman. Accordingly, he sent word to Prithvi Singh that he would like to seal their long friendship with a marriage. However, he also added the warning that if Prithvi Singh did not agree to the proposal, he would be compelled to consent. The emissary intimated that a huge army was ready to make war with Chenji.

'This message made Prithvi Singh shake in fury. He called for his council. No councillor dared to give him advice. Refusing the proposal meant getting ready for war. Was it feasible to fight an army of three thousand with a force of three hundred soldiers? But no one had the courage to tell the king to give his daughter in marriage to the Nawab.

'At this juncture, Sukumaran got up to make a suggestion. He had the courage to say that the Nawab's demand must be rejected. "Let the Nawab march against us. We have the power to withstand a siege for six months. Shivaji Maharaj of Maharashtra has vowed to protect Hinduism. He will certainly come to help us if we ask him. I will personally go and bring him here," he said. The delighted Prithvi Singh agreed to send Sukumaran to Maharashtra.

200

'On the night of the full moon in the month of Maasi, Sukumaran met Malati and bid her farewell as he started on his mission to Shivaji Maharaj. He said that his success in that mission would make the king happy enough to give his consent to their marriage. Malati shared his faith. And yet the parting was full of sorrow. That was when she asked Sukumaran not to forget her, and he swore that he would not forget her through all his subsequent births.

'A few days after Sukumaran left, his ministers counselled Prithvi Singh to relent. "Shivaji's coming to our aid is a pipe dream. Sukumaran is a fool. He has no worldy wisdom. It is not even certain that he will meet Shivaji. It is better to make peace with the Nawab," they said.

'Malati made a mistake. One day, when she found the king in good humour, she disclosed her love and begged her father to let her marry Sukumaran. This wrought a complete change of heart in Prithvi Singh. He was furious that under the pretext of teaching music, the man had captured his daughter's heart. He felt enraged at the thought of marriage between the princess and the son of a tutor. It would be better to give her in marriage to the Nawab instead. Hadn't many great Rajput kings shown the way by giving their daughters in marriage to Mughal rulers? Why shouldn't he do the same thing? With her beauty and wit, perhaps his daughter would turn into another Nurjahan. Thus ran the

201

thoughts of the greedy old man. Heedless of his daughter's wishes, he conveyed his consent to the Nawab.

'This decision was torture to Malati. To marry another was to betray Sukumaran, who had sworn to love her forever. It was something she could not even dream of doing. She begged and pleaded, but to no avail. Finally, one night she left the castle to go to the temple of Kali, the guardian deity of the fort. Praying to the goddess, she jumped into the deep tank beside the temple and died.

'This calamitous event caused Prithvi Singh to go mad. He had no other children and the Nawab captured the fort very easily.

'Crossing many hurdles, Sukumaran did finally manage to meet the great warrior in person. Shivaji could not dismiss his plea. Since he had long wanted to march southwards, he arrived with a huge army and captured the fort in a single day. But Sukumaran did not enter the fort. He lost all interest in worldly affairs when he learnt Malati's fate. With a tambura made from a gourd, he wandered through the land, singing of the transcience of worldly life and the greatness of love.

'I am the same Sukumaran who has returned to this place in my seventh incarnation . . . Well, it's getting rather late. Shouldn't you leave now? Won't your friends be waiting for you?' Kumaraswami asked.

True, it was very late. It could be 7.30 or even 8.00 p.m. Though I strained my ears, I could not hear the honking from the car. I noticed that Kumaraswami was more agitated than before and that he wanted me to leave. Could his tale be true? It was the day of the full moon. Would that enchantress from the spirit world appear here again? Would my eyes be able to see her? I was scared, but I didn't want to quit that place without knowing the truth.

'You have left out something important. What happened to Malati after she jumped into the tank? What was she doing until you returned in your seventh incarnation?' I asked.

'Oh, did I forget to tell you ? My mind often gets muddled,' said Kumaraswami.

The account that followed was so incredible as to make everything else seem commonplace. It was also jumbled and contradictory in some aspects. Therefore let me summarize the whole and put it in some kind of coherent order.

Malati became unconscious as she jumped into the temple tank. When she recovered, she found herself in the arms of Mother Kali! She heard Kali say, 'Child! Why have you done this? Won't people curse me for accepting a human sacrifice?' Malati did not realise that she had become a spirit. She thought she had been saved from death by Mother Kali. So she gripped Kali's feet firmly and wailed, 'Mother, I will let

203

you go only if you grant me a boon.' When the goddess promised, Malati pleaded, 'Mother ! Do I have to ask? Don't you know? The only boon I crave is to wed Sukumaran.'

Then Kali made her realise her true state. Since Malati had become a spirit without a flesh-and-blood body, Kali explained that she would have to be born again to attain Sukumaran as her husband. But Malati did not let go of the Mother's feet. 'What is the guarantee that I will retain memory of this birth in the next? I must attain Sukumaran with all my memories of this life intact,' was her stubborn demand. 'Then you must wait for three thousand years and roam through these hills as a restless spirit. Every second will seem an era. Will you accept that?' asked Kali. 'I will wait through all the ages,' was Malati's answer. 'All right, then I will grant you the boon you crave. With your memories of this life intact, you will attain Sukumaran in his seventh incarnation after this one. During each of those births, he will visit this place once, but will not be able to see you. In the seventh birth, you will become visible to his eyes. You will wed each other in my presence,' Kali assured her.

From that moment Malati wandered through the Chenji region as a spirit. She watched every single thing that happened in the fort. But no one saw her. And as Mother Kali warned her, every second passed like a whole era. Her love and longing for Sukumaran mounted through the years.

As she did not have a human form, she could neither shed tears nor lament, nor find any other means of consolation. All the longing swelled and seethed inside her.

As Kali had promised, Sukumaran did visit Chenji once during each subsequent birth. Those were moments of intense agony for Malati. She recognised him each time. But he had no inkling of her presence. And yet, each time he came, he did experience an indescribable anguish and hesitated to leave the place.

Finally, during his visit in his seventh incarnation, Malati's desire was fulfilled. She was able to appear before him and converse with him. When she prompted him, Kumaraswami too slowly recovered his memories of that previous life.

'That's the end of my tale. Isn't it getting late for you?' said Kumaraswami as he stood up.

I too got up and said, 'Aren't you coming with me? Surely you are not going to stay here?'

Kumaraswami looked at the round moon rising in the sky. 'Don't you see that it is full moon?'

That was when I asked him the question, which had been seething in my heart. 'Do you expect your Malati to arrive now?'

Kumaraswami laughed. 'You don't believe a word of what I've said!'

At that precise moment, from the distance came the

tinkle of anklets and the jingle of bangles. My hair stood on end. I began to sweat all over. I turned towards the direction from which the sounds came. A little ahead of us, behind the undergrowth, the form of a woman could be discerned. As far as I could see, she was attired like a bride. In two bounds, Kumaraswami was beside her.

My body began to tremble violently. At the same time a car horn honked loudly from the road. It must have been honking for some time. But I heard it only then.

I walked fast towards the car. I was afraid to take a backward look. My fears accelerated every second. I began to run.

My friends came to meet me a furlong away from the road. I pulled myself together when I saw them. Still, they knew that I had fled in fear. They caught me by the hand and took me back to the car. I gained courage when the car began to move. I asked why they were so late. They told me that the car had problems starting, it had taken a long time to get it going again. And yet, they had reached the ruins a half-hour before. When despite repeated honking, I had not appeared, they had come looking for me with some trepidation.

They wanted to know why I had tarried so long. Did I lose my way? I said yes. I was afraid they would not believe me if I related my experience. They would laugh at me.

In Minnalur, the next village after Chenji, we found a huge pandal put up across the whole street. We had to turn back and find another way out. When we enquired about the pandal, we were told that it was for the wedding of the daughter of the zamindar, due to take place next week.

Hearing this reference to a wedding, I blurted out that a wedding was to take place that night at the Chenji Fort. After that, my friends would not rest until they dragged out every detail of my experience. Just as I expected, they did not believe the entire tale. But they did wonder if there was some measure of truth in it, as they had seen me fleeing the fort with shaking limbs.

A couple of days later, back in Madras, I began to doubt my own experience. I engaged myself in other tasks to try and forget it. But three days after my return, I was once again reminded of Chenji by a news item published in the corner of an evening newspaper:

A Distressing Incident

The famous Chenji Fort was the scene of a distressing incident last full moon night. A young man and a young woman were found dead before the tank of the Mother Goddess. The post-mortem report states that death was due to poison.

The young man Kumaraswami was a teacher at the local elementary school, under orders of transfer to another village. The woman was the only daughter of zamindar Seshachala Reddiar. She was to be married next week. Rumour has it that Kumaraswami and the young woman had been in love with each other. The zamindar had refused his consent to their marriage, and arranged his daughter's marriage into a wealthy family, leading to this calamitous event. Distressed as they are over this sad end, the locals are also amazed by the couple's display of such deep attachment in these fickle times . . .

I am generally reputed to be hard-hearted, but this report brought tears to my eyes. Not only did I grieve over the untimely death of the young lovers, I also lamented the loss of a rare creator of fiction.

Fool! Couldn't he have told me the real story? If he had, wouldn't I have saved him with sage advice, drawing on apt parallels and examples? 'Silly fellow!' I would have said. 'Love and passion are but three days' madness! Of what use is it to give up your life? At least, dying for your country makes some sense!'

# V

EENAI BHAVANI

'Veenai Bhavani'
*Kalki* (1942)

# 1

*I*t was around nine o'clock at night. Black clouds filled the sky. There was a slight drizzle. In the dim light of the shaded street lamps, the sky seemed to be shedding tears from a sorrow too deep for words.

I simply couldn't bear the gloomy sight. I came into the house. My mind was sunk in dejection. I shut the windows against both aggravations and switched the lights on. I picked up a book, hoping that it would bring about a change of mood.

Readers may wish to know why I felt depressed. Aren't there reasons galore for depression? The state of the world and of the country can furnish any number of reasons for low spirits. As if these were not enough, a report in the evening newspaper exhausted whatever reserves of zest I may have had.

There had been a train accident somewhere between Kudalur and Chidambaram. Having left Egmore last night, the Boat Mail had met with a serious accident. The cause was yet unknown. But the city heard several versions of the story. The official explanation was that the tracks had been washed away in a sudden and heavy downpour. Rumour had it that someone had deliberately sabotaged the tracks because a high-ranking official of the Railways was travelling by the train. There were endless rumours about the numbers of the dead.

I was not as badly shaken by the news that a hundred, maybe even two hundred, persons had met their deaths in the accident. But I felt as if the train had crashed right over me when I scanned the long death list and came across a certain name.

Readers may remember Iyampettai Kandappan. He was the tavil player who had told me the story of the nadaswaram maestro Sivakozhundu. Seeing his name among the dead hit me hard.

For God has made us like that. We don't react when we hear of twenty thousand people dying in a volcanic eruption in America. Yet we feel miserable when we hear of the death of someone we know personally.

Should Iyampettai Kandappan have met such a tragic end? What a wonderful man he was! What a patriot! So good and conscientious! With such affection for his friends! A true connoisseur! The sound of a horsecab halting in front of my house disturbed my reflections. 'Who can it be at this hour?' I wondered with some distaste. My mind was in no fit state for me to receive anyone.

A second later the front door was opened. I wouldn't have been more astounded if I had found Adolf Hitler or General Tojo on my doorstep. For the man who stood there was none other than Iyampettai Kandappan.

'Don't be afraid! It is I myself in the flesh, not my ghost!' When I heard Kandappan's voice, amazement turned to overwhelming delight.

'Welcome, welcome!' I cried as I took him by the hand and made him take a seat.

'What happened? How did you manage to escape from the train accident? I was terribly upset to see your name in the newspaper. How could they make such a mistake? Shame on them!' I went on and on in excitement.

'Thank God I didn't board that train! I had reserved my seat in advance. My tavil and luggage had been loaded on to the compartment but I myself reached the station two minutes after the train had left. I was lucky . . .'

'Your name must have been on the passengers' list. Seeing that and your tavil, the press obviously decided to send you straight to heaven!'

'I think so.'

'Won't your people be worried? Why didn't you go home today?' I asked him.

'I've sent them a telegram. I thought I should give you a fright before I went home.'

'You tried to scare me?'

'Yes. Didn't you frighten us in the same manner in one of your stories? This is my revenge.'

213

'Such things can happen in stories. Not in real life,' I said.

'You are completely wrong,' Kandappan averred.

'How can you be so absolutely sure of that?'

'Because I have seen such a thing happen in real life.'

'What thing?'

'Danger arose because a man presumed dead made a sudden appearance.'

'What kind of danger?'

'Danger to life.'

I knew then that Kandappan had come with the specific intent of relating an interesting incident.

'Tell me all about it, I'd love to hear it. My mind is very unsettled today. I feel extremely depressed. Perhaps, if I listen to your story . . .'

'. . . This is not a story to arouse enthusiasm. It is steeped in grief. Perhaps we'll keep it for another day . . .'

'Not at all. You must listen to a sad story especially when you feel depressed. So tell me now . . .'

## 2

Kandappa Pillai began all his tales with a question. He made no exception this time. He cleared his throat in preparation and asked me, 'Do you recall having heard of Poonthottam Bhavani?'

I recognized the name but as if through the mists of a

214

previous birth. I remembered having listened to two or three gramophone 'plates' by her. But Kandappa Pillai did not wait for me to prod my memory any further. He went on.

'Thirty years ago, Poonthottam Bhavani was a celebrated name. She was also known as Veenai Bhavani. When she sang with the veena on her lap, it was as if the goddess Saraswati herself donned a human form and appeared before us. You could compare her voice only to the ringing resonance of the veena's string when her fingers plucked it. The sound she evoked from the veena found its match only in her voice. Her concerts were held before assemblies of thousands of people who listened in rapt silence. They lost themselves in her music.

'Bhavani performed frequently in temples, particularly at the Tiruvarur temple during festival time. Nowdays we see atheism gaining ground. Rationalists' movements and Self-Respect movements are making things worse for the world. On top of all this, we have the advent of cinema. There are very few left who will conduct temple festivals with care and solicitude.

'But in those days people found their enjoyment only in the rituals and festivities connected to the temples. From twenty miles around people would throng in multitudes to attend them.

'At festival time music concerts were held in the kalyana mandapam of the temple. Every concert drew capacity crowds, but Poonthottam Bhavani's recitals broke all records. "As great a crowd as at Poonthottam Bhavani's concerts" became a common phrase of the times.

'You can imagine the din and racket at such colossal gatherings. But Bhavani's fingers had only to touch the strings, she had only to raise her head slightly and align her sweet voice to their pitch. The noise subsided at once. As Bhavani's mellifluous voice, accompanied by the veena's resonance rose, and the audience fell silent, there was a hint of other-worldly magic.

'I never missed a chance to attend Bhavani's concerts. And I did often get to hear her. I found that Bhavani's concerts were also held at many of the weddings and temple functions to which I was invited in my professional capacity. Tears would come to my eyes whenever I listened to her music. I would drop my head down, pretending to have a headache, so that the others did not laugh at my response. You ask me the reason for those tears? I don't know myself. Were they tears of bliss? Or evoked by fears that so marvellous an outpouring may be shortlived? Can such music last long? Can the world bear such divine ecstasy? A few others would worry about the effects of the evil eye on the artiste. I invariably went to meet Bhavani after every concert

216

and told her, "Thangachi, ask your mother to take some ritual precautions against the evil eye."

'And Bhavani's mother did take every care of her daughter. Yet misfortune could not be averted.

'Bhavani's mother Poonthottam Brahadambal had inherited the great wealth of many generations. She was also famous for her virtuous conduct. She had a relationship with a single man of distinguished status. She was like a chaste wife to him. When he died, she turned her mind to God and to acts of piety.

'The daughter had the same qualities. She came to the stage with the sacred ash on her forehead. She sang nothing but songs of devotion. Elaborate ritual worship was offered daily in their home. Even wagging tongues declared that Bhavani was lost in a spiritual quest.

'Brahadambal wished to get her daughter married to a respectable man. But Bhavani insisted that she had vowed to remain single, and like the saint-poet Andal, she too would find her refuge only in the feet of the Lord.

'Neither mother nor daughter realized her ambition. Things went awry, all because of a few casual words spoken by one man to another.

'Once, when Bhavani concluded her concert at the Tiruvarur temple and was about to get into her coach, she happened quite by chance to overhear a man talking to his friend as they walked past her. "You keep harping on her music! Never mind the music. What about her looks, the charm that oozes from her face?"

'When Bhavani heard this she couldn't help but burst into laughter. The speaker turned to see who laughed. He was terribly embarrassed to find Bhavani standing close by. Bhavani got into her coach quickly and drove away.

'Well, this turned out to be fateful. Why should that particular man have spoken just those words in the dark as Bhavani was getting into her carriage? Why should his remarks have fallen on her ears?

'As soon as Bhavani went home she asked her mother why she had forgotten to pack her handkerchief for the concert that day. The mother was silent, dismissing it as a meaningless query.

'"It was very stuffy in the hall. I perspired all the time," explained Bhavani. "But listen to this, Amma, my face was dripping with sweat. A man who saw it thought I oozed charm!" she laughed. Later mother and daughter would often narrate this incident to me. But what began in fun and laughter ended in disaster.

## 3

'I knew the man. He was a landowner in a village called Tumbaivanam near Mannargudi. Gopalsami Mudaliar was quite young. In fact I had played the tavil at his wedding. He had been married for five or six years when Bhavani saw him. He had children as well.

'Fate decided to bring him and Bhavani together. I don't know how they met again, or how their relationship grew. When fate ordains something, it also clears the way. It was rumoured that Bhavani had strayed from her spiritual quest. And Tumbaivanam Gopalsami Mudaliar's name came to be bandied about throughout Thanjavur district.

'These rumours brought me little comfort. You know my views. I believe that the perpetuation of the devadasi community and profession is a social evil which must be totally abolished. Why should things have taken such a turn? Couldn't Bhavani have entered into a respectable marriage? I felt very sorry for Gopalsami Mudaliar's wife and children. More than ever I became anxious that this connection would have an adverse effect on Bhavani's divine music.

'Thank God, that did not happen, Gopalsami Mudaliar was a true connoisseur. He was also extremely proud of Bhavani's musical gifts. Well do I remember what he said to me once. "The Creator did not make Bhavani as he made other human beings. He has shaped her out of Kalyani and Mohanam and Senjurutti. Wait and see. When Bhavani dies, her body will melt and waft away into ragams."

'"That may be," I answered him. "But you and I

219

won't see it. Bhavani will sing for many years after our time."

'God has not given us the power to see into the future. If he had, would there be any sorrow in the world? Or joy for that matter?

'Yes, I was describing Bhavani's music. It scaled newer peaks. But to my ears accustomed to her style, many surprising changes were discernible. One concert was not like another. One day the melody would swell in exhilaration. You could hear in it the gladness of birdsong welcoming the dawn. And the joyous clamour of the waves as they rose to greet the full moon. On other occasions, the listener's heart was filled with melancholy without cause. The poignant wail of the child torn from its mother and the devotee's anguished cry for the Lord were alike audible in that music. You wondered if she played on the strings of the veena or on the heart strings of the listeners.

'At first I found this puzzling and mysterious. Slowly I understood something of the matter.

'What we term love and affection are inexplicable phenomena. What do human beings attain through love? Pain? Joy? Indescribable misery? Immeasurable rapture?

'Whatever I heard about Bhavani and Tumbaivanam Mudaliar raised these questions in my mind. It was impossible to say whether they had more days of happiness together or

220

spent their time in suffering and squabbles. Her mother told me she thought Bhavani was bewitched. Sometimes she would snarl at everyone and throw a tantrum over trifles. She would shout and scream. Or alternately, she would sit still for hours, her face unwashed, hair uncombed . . .

'At other times her behaviour was exactly the opposite. She would adorn herself splendidly and indulge in excited laughter. When I heard all this I understood somewhat the reasons for the changes in her music. Therefore, when her mother asked me if she should call an exorcist to come and take a look at Bhavani, I had no hesitation in answering her, "You don't need chants and spells. In a little while, everything will be all right."

## 4

'Two or three years went by. In that period Tumbaivanam Mudaliar's financial affairs became a mess. His enemies increased in number. It was to be expected that many rich landowners would have their eyes on Bhavani. Now they ganged together and vowed to destroy Gopalsami Mudaliar.

'At first it was a court case in connection with the temple committee. Gopalsami Mudaliar was one of the three trustees of the temple. Not content with excluding Mudaliar from the committee's transactions, the other trustees insulted him

221

in public during the temple festival. The enraged Gopalsami went to court.

'That was the beginning of a whole chain of civil and criminal cases in which he became involved. The neighbouring landlords and aristocrats went about determined to bring Gopalsami to ruin. Gopalsami's debts mounted day by day. Every year, he sold yet another piece of land.

'Once while attending the temple festival at Tumbaivanam, I called at Mudaliar's home. His wife belonged to a village close to Iyampettai. I knew her well. Poor thing! She was plunged in misery. "Kandappa, that Poonthottam bitch is the cause of all our misfortunes," she wept. I felt extremely sorry for her. I deplored the existence of the devadasi community. I resolved to make known to Bhavani the deep-seated anger I felt the next time I went to Tiruvarur.

'But when I saw Bhavani's condition, all hostile thoughts vanished. She was grief personified. She repeatedly blamed herself for Gopalsami's tribulations. I had to console her by reiterating that it was not her fault at all; there was nothing she could do about it.

'"Anna! I tell him to cut off all connections with his land, house and property and to make his permanent home here. But he doesn't listen to me. Can't you persuade him? It has become a daily ritual for him to go to court every morning! Why should he get involved in all these legal hassles when four generations can live off the property we have here? Who else is there to enjoy it all?" said Bhavani.

'"Talk sense, Thangachi, he's a man, isn't he? Doesn't he have some self-respect? Will he run away from home and town simply because people wantonly create problems for him? Even if he agrees to your proposal, what about his wife and children?" I reproved her.

'After this Bhavani would ask me frequently about his wife and children.

'I spoke my mind to Bhavani's mother. "Why invite notoriety? Throughout the district gossip has it that Bhavani is bringing a respectable family to ruin."

'"Let the people talk. It would be a great sin to separate them. If that happens, my daughter will not stay alive."

'"How many people have mouthed the same dialogue? Haven't we heard it all?" I shrugged.

'"You don't know Bhavani's nature," was her answer.

'Then I enquired about the state of their relationship. Was it just as stormy as before? I learnt that Bhavani's personality had undergone a total transformation. She was now the image of tranquillity. In direct contrast, Gopalsami Mudaliar had became highly temperamental. Moreover, he was tormented by jealous doubts. I was surprised by the vicissitudes of human nature. Why should Bhavani love a man so dearly and without any cause or compulsion? That a man should doubt a woman who gave him heartfelt devotion of her own accord aroused my anger and aversion. I went quietly away. I had no wish to get involved further.

'For about a year after that, personal problems kept me busy and I could not visit Tiruvarur. I did go once to offer my condolences to Bhavani when her mother died. I stopped going there because I felt I should not become embroiled in what was really no business of mine.

'But I did often hear that things were going from bad to worse for Tumbaivanam Mudaliar. They said he would become bankrupt if he lost the case then being heard in the Madras High Court.

'It was also at that time that we heard the report of a terrible train accident. The train had derailed between Vizhupuram and Kudalur. Three compartments had been reduced to debris. Forty or fifty persons had died on the spot. I had been an avid reader of the newspapers even in those days. Anxiously did I await the arrival of the *Swadesamitran* to follow the details of the dreadful accident. A list of the names of those who had perished was published the day after the accident. Imagine my feelings when I came across Tumbaivanam Mudaliar's name there. It was Poonthottam Bhavani who came immediately to mind. The poor girl was stranded, alone in the world, losing both her mother and her lover within the same year. What would happen to her now?

'I also thought of Gopalsami Mudaliar's wife and children. Poor things! All their wealth had been lost in fighting legal battles. Would they now be reduced to utter penury?

'I had to go to Mannargudi the week after. From there I made a trip to Tumbaivanam. I couldn't bear to see Mudaliar's wife. She was totally crushed by despair. The children were a pitiful sight. Luckily, their grandfather and grandmother had come from their village to take care of the children and to console the mother. "What to do, my dear," they told her. "You have to accept your destiny. For the sake of the children you must take hold of yourself and carry on with life." They made sure she did not starve herself. I too did my best to put some heart into her before I left.

'After meeting them, I felt the urge to visit Bhavani as well. I went straight to Tiruvarur. It was with great trepidation that I made my way to her house. How could I bear to see her drowned in grief? How would I find the words to speak to her, much less condole with her?

'But when I saw Bhavani my anxieties were dispelled. Because she was neither tear-stained nor confined to her bed as I expected and feared. No agonized shrieks when she saw me. She appeared quiet normal. She even welcomed my eagerly.

'Did I say my anxieties were dispelled? Yes, they were. But

I also felt deep disappointment. Finally the world was proved right in upbraiding the devadasi community for its callousness. What a tremendous contrast between the wails of the wedded wife and this casual welcoming of chance visitors!

'I did not reveal my true feelings. I offered routine words of sympathy, more to discharge my duty than for anything else. As I took my leave of her Bhavani said, "Anna! I am going to give a concert before the sanctum of the goddess in the temple, on Friday evening during the Navaratri festival. You must come to hear me."

'I was flabbergasted. A concert? So soon? "Thangachi, do you have to perform this year? Can't you wait till next year?" I asked her.

'"No, Anna, I had agreed to give that concert. They have printed my name in the festival invitation. I don't want to back out now."

'My indignation was directed at both Bhavani and the temple trustees.

'"I will come if I can," I replied.

'"Don't say that, Anna! This may be my last concert. You must certainly be there."

'My heart melted at these words. "Why do you say that? Whatever happens, your music must continue to grow and flourish," said I and left, promising to attend the concert.

226

## 5

'I did go to Tiruvarur on the Friday during Navaratri as I had promised. I reached her house just as she was setting out for the concert. I was stunned to see her magnificently dressed in silks and jewels. She looked like a bride about to enter the wedding hall.

'Bhavani was endowed with great natural beauty. Adorned as she was, she seemed a celestial nymph. Had Rambha, Urvashi, Menaka or Tilottama left the heavens and come down to the earth? But I cannot tell you how that vision tormented me.

'"Anna, so you did come!" Bhavani smiled at me.

'I was outraged. But I answered with outward calm, "Yes, Thangachi, I did."

'"Anna, I had been expecting you since morning. Never mind. You must come straight home after the concert. It is about a crucial matter. You must not let me down."

'"All right, Thangachi!"

'"I swear it on your head. It is important. You must not fail me," said she and got into her carriage.

'I had never heard Bhavani talk in this manner. Clearly something significant was afoot. I went to the temple in a thoughtful mood.

'I have heard any number of concerts in my life. I have

heard famous musicians, both men and women. But never have I heard anything like the concert Bhavani gave at the temple on that Navaratri Friday. Her voice was as mellifluous as honey. Nectar flowed from the strings of the veena when her fingers plucked them. But there was something in it above and beyond the allure of melody and musicianship. It evoked the pain of an incredible sweetness. There was pin-drop silence in the assembly. You couldn't even hear the sounds of breathing. Nor were there the usual cries of appreciation— "Aah!", "Bhesh", "Shabash!" The crowd savoured her divine music as if bound by a spell of enchantment.

'Finally when Bhavani sang the lines of the Tiruvachakam "Paal ninaindootum taayinum saala parindu . . ." in ragam Khambhoji, I looked at the figure of the Divine Mother inside the sanctum. I was surprised that her stone image did not melt as she listened to Bhavani's song. I thought I saw teardrops in the eyes of the goddess. I wiped my own eyes, chiding myself for yielding to such hallucinations.

'I looked around me. On all four sides of the hall, people had packed themselves to stand like solid walls. Quite by accident, my eyes fell upon a face right at the back and in a corner. It was partly hidden by a huge makeshift turban covering half the forehead. A pair of big green-tinted spectacles indicated that the wearer suffered from some ailment of the eye. For some reason I found my own glance and attention repeatedly returning to that face. I became less attentive to the music. I wondered to whom the face belonged. Somehow he seemed familiar . . .

'In a flash I knew the truth. My whole body began to quake in a panic. I had a premonition of impending disaster. Since I was sitting at the back, it was easy for me to get up and make my way behind the row of standing listeners to where the man with the green glasses stood.

'The concert was over. The man made a swift exit from the assembly, ahead of the others. I followed him. As soon as we came out of the temple and reached a quiet spot I grabbed his hands and exclaimed, "What's this! Why the disguise?"

'Gopalsami Mudaliar flung my hands off. But when he saw who I was, he burst into bitter speech. "Yes, Kandappa, yes. It is a disguise. The whole world is in disguise. Didn't you see how your dear sister had disguised herself today? She had worn a different disguise before this!"

'"No, you don't know all the circumstances. Bhavani told me this was her last concert. That is why she sang like one possessed," I tried to calm him down.

'"Kandappa, are you trying to fool me? You think I am an innocent child? Fantastic music! Fabulous concert . . . ! How did she have the heart to do it? God willed the train crash only to open my eyes!"

229

'To change the subject, I fired questions at him. "Certainly it was God himself who brought you back safe and sound. Tell me about this miracle. Why did the news report make such a mistake? How did you escape from the accident? Where were you all these days?"

'"I will give you all the details later. Enough to make a novel. By God's grace, I was saved at death's door. For ten days I lay unconscious in the hospital. Then I saw my name included in the death list published in the old newspapers. I wished to see people's reactions to my death, especially of those who swore they would jump into the funeral pyre with me. How would they have taken it? That's why I came dressed like this. Now I have seen it all," said he with revulsion.

'We had been walking on the street as we talked. "Forget all those things. But where do you intend to go now?" I asked him.

'"Why, I'm going there. Don't think I will thrash her or kill her. I shall merely congratulate her on her stunning performance and go away. That's all. If you like, you can come along and watch," said Gopalsami Mudaliar.

'So we walked together to Bhavani's house. Her horse-drawn carriage stood outside. She was home. I wanted to go in alone and prepare her. But Gopalsami Mudaliar would not allow it. He shoved me aside and strode into the room first. As we entered, we saw Bhavani with a cup of milk held to her lips. When she saw the man with the huge turban and green glasses, she stood rooted to the spot in amazement. Mudaliar removed his glasses and turban. I saw a terrible change come over her face. My heart stopped beating.

'I don't know for how long the three of us remained transfixed. I came to only when I saw Bhavani crumple and collapse on the floor. Gopalsami was there before me. He lifted her and put her on his lap. For a few minutes I looked helplessly around. Then I ran to fetch the doctor. When I returned with the doctor there was no doubt about it. It was half an hour since Bhavani had breathed her last.'

## 6

Kandappa Pillai broke off at this point. He had narrated the whole story with so much feeling and lucidity, it seemed every incident was taking place right before our eyes. I was deeply moved. I was silent for a while. There was nothing to say.

Then I remembered where our conversation had begun. And I said, 'So Bhavani was petrified because she mistook the sudden appearance of Gopalsami Mudaliar for his ghost. What did you do after that?'

'What more could we do? I got the doctor to write out a certificate of death caused by sudden shock. Gopalsami

Mudaliar and I performed the final rites. Poor man, there was no end to his grief.'

'Did the Mudaliar realize at least then that Bhavani's love had remained pure and untarnished? Did he come to value the depth of her feelings for him?' I asked.

'How could he know? Even though he grieved for her, he also believed that Bhavani had died from shock, knowing that he had seen through her deception. His distrust was mitigated somewhat when he learnt that Bhavani had left her wealth and property to his children. Her will was with her lawyer.'

'Really!' I exclaimed in surprise. I could see from the expression on Kandappa Pillai's face that there was more to come.

'Things had followed their natural course. Why did you then have to get a doctor's certificate?' I asked.

'As a safeguard against police harassment which is usual in such cases of sudden death. That's all. I didn't tell Gopalsami Mudaliar the truth. Only the doctor and I knew,' said he.

I thought there was still something left to be told. 'What was the real cause of death?' I asked.

'It is more than twenty-five years since it happened. I don't suppose there is any harm in disclosing the truth now. Didn't I run behind Mudaliar when Bhavani fell to the floor?

232

I noticed a letter on the teapoy, lying beside the cup she had drunk from. Seeing my name on it, I quickly snatched it and tucked it out of sight. I read it under the street lamp when I went to fetch the doctor. Here it is,' said Kandappa Pillai and gave me a letter. The paper was old and frayed. The script, written in a beautiful hand, had dimmed with age. It said:

My dear Kandappa Anna,

I don't wish to live without the man I love more than my life. Today I perform my last concert. I have powdered the diamonds from the ring he gifted to me with such tender affection. I will swallow that powder as soon as I return from the concert. I have bequeathed half my property to the temple and the other half to his children. My will is with Advocate ——Iyer. Please forgive me if I do wrong. I cannot live without him.

Yours,

Bhavani

I read that letter two or three times and asked, 'Why didn't you show it to Gopalsami Mudaliar?'

'What's the use of telling him about it? He was already a man shattered. If he had known about the letter, he too might have taken his life. Or he might have ceased to have any attachment for his wife and children. Why cause the break-up of a family? No, I did not tell him the truth.'

After a pause Kandappa Pillai got up and took his leave of me. I returned the letter to him.

He opened the front door and went away. The breeze blew cold. The black sky drizzled softly.

# MADATEVAN'S SPRING

'Madatevan Sunai'
*Kalki* (1950)

# Preface

*I* once had to travel through Ramanathapuram district to attend an Annual Day function. It was a time when news came in from all over the country of railway tracks sliding away from under trains and derailing them. Still, I stopped worrying when I learnt that an honourable minister was travelling in my train. Don't our ministers follow the words of Tiruvalluvar—that vigilance, education and courage are the attributes of those who reign over the realm? With a minister ever-awake, who would dare to tamper with the rails? Could the God of Death himself draw nigh?

The train halted where the woods grew on either side at a little distance past the Kattuppakkam station, because a train coming in the opposite direction had somehow managed to slide off the tracks! Thank God! If this fate had overtaken my train! Surely it was God's will that I survive, perhaps to perform some vital tasks. The same God who once prevented the death of that valiant hero Lord Clive when he tried to shoot himself, must have saved me! Who knows when, and where, I was destined to build or destroy an empire?

After halting at Kattupakkam for four-and-a-half hours, our train began to move, but at a slower pace. It reached Madurai not at 8 a.m. as scheduled, but at 12.30 p.m. That was when I came to know that the Honourable Minister,

237

who had fallen asleep at Egmore station, had woken up only at Dindigul. Good I didn't put all my trust in the minister, reserving some of my faith for God.

By that time we were so late that we could no longer count on the train reaching our destination in time for us to make it to the function. So we hired a car at Madurai to continue on the journey. We had engine trouble on the way. The vehicle spewed smoke from its front and rear.

'In this dry land which barely yields water enough for humans and animals, where can we find the water to satisfy the demands of a car?' I expressed my anxiety.

'Soon we will come to Madatevan's spring. It will surely have all the water we need,' my fellow traveller from the Pandya region replied.

Soon we did reach Madatevan's spring, on the top of a small, black boulder beside the road, with not the slightest trace of greenery anywhere. Below the boulder were the remnants of some structure, possibly an old fort which might once have stood there and fallen into ruin in later times. Of the fort, not even a single wall remained intact. All that could be seen were a few ravaged stones of the fort's foundation.

In a region parched for miles around, the presence of sweet, clear water in the spring of black rock seemed a great mystery to me. What miraculous power nature wields! Once we got over our amazement at finding such a spring there, our attention fastened on a black stone placed vertically beside the boulder. A small spear was embedded in the ground next to it. From the sandalwood paste, kumkumam, oil stains and the flowers strewn over them, I could see that the stone and spear were objects of worship.

I had no doubt that there existed a tale about Madatevan's spring. But who had the time then to go seeking it? The Annual Function was looming over us. We left as soon as the car's thirst was quenched.

The tale I tell here is what I gathered from the people living in that region on a subsequent visit to the spot. I have added some details and conjectures. Even if you don't like the additions, I hope you will enjoy the story.

## 1

A hundred and fifty years ago, there was a small fort at the bottom of Arjunan Hill to which that sweet spring belonged. Once upon a time, Arjunan came down south on a pilgrimage, and performed a penance on that hill. That was when his father poured a pot of water down from the heavens to quench his son's thirst. The water that remained turned into a spring. That was how the hill came to be called after Arjunan. This is the legend about the hill. But what we are looking into is why the water came to be named Madatevan's spring.

239

A few thousand years after Arjunan performed his penance, one of the Pandya kings built a fort below the hill. Ravaged by the passage of time, the fort was in ruins even during the period when our tale took place. People paid little attention to it. After executing Veera Pandya Kattabomman of Panchalankurichi, the white men of the British East India Company ordered the destruction of all the forts of the chieftains in Pandya country. But they did not insist on destroying this fort. Already in ruins, it could not be used in warfare, nor was it possible for many people to find shelter in it.

An old man called Karuppiah Servai and his beloved daughter Velammal were the only inhabitants of the fort. The fort had offered protection to wayfarers from the robbers who plagued the region then. The chieftain of Sivagangai had established Karuppiah there with his family, and paid him a grant. As a young man, Karuppiah had been strong and brave. With a staff in his hand, he could single-handedly put ten robbers to flight. Sometimes travellers stayed overnight at the fort. They rewarded Karuppiah suitably for providing them with lodging and protection.

All that was in the old days. Everything turned upside down after the men of the British company started levying taxes for the Nawab of Arcot. Karuppiah stopped getting his grant. His dear wife died leaving him and his little

Velammal destitute. No longer was there any need to fear
robbers. Since the white men had stripped everything bare
in daylight robbery, what did the robbers have left to steal?
And how could Servai and his daughter eke out a living?

The spring on top of Arjunan Hill aided father and
daughter in getting by. Normally, the pool had water lapping
at the brim during the monsoon and winter. A little waterfall
flowed from it into the fort, over a side wall, and found its
way out to the bottom of the hill. This enabled a young
man to grow his crops there. Sometimes he planted ragi; at
other times he grew cucumbers. He was a hard worker. His
land was always lush and green. Travellers on the highway
would invariably stop to gaze at his garden, some with delight,
others with envy.

Karuppiah belonged to the latter category. The old man
burned with envy to see the labours of Madatevan bring
such rich returns. He knew he did not have the strength to
work as hard. Age, poverty and liquor had weakened his
iron frame. Was it not natural for him to feel bad to see a
newcomer doing so well, when he and his daughter could
scarcely make ends meet? Soon, he began to quarrel with
the young man over the water from the spring. He threatened
to dam the water flowing through his fort. Madatevan was
not cowed. 'Does the spring belong to you? Is the fort your
personal property? God created the spring. The ruined fort

belongs to the chieftain of Sivagangai. Try to stop the water and see if I don't get permission from the chieftain to make free use of it!'

'What right has the chieftain here? Does he pay me? Those days are gone forever. Even so great a Pandya warrior as Kattabomman was hanged on a tamarind tree by the white men of the company. What can this chieftain do to me? The fort is mine. I will stop the water if I like,' growled the old man.

Velammal, who had eavesdropped on this exchange, went down that evening to Madatevan's garden. For a while, they stood simply gazing at each other. It was not easy to speak. There was a lump in Velammal's throat. Tears stood in her eyes. At that very moment, the full moon rose in the eastern sky. The moonbeams transformed Velammal's tears into sparkling pearls.

As soon as he saw this, Madatevan became Velammal's slave.

'Woman! Why are you here alone and at this time? What will your father say if he knows?' he asked.

Before this, they had met and talked to each other occasionally but always from a distance. Velammal had never entered Madatevan's garden.

'I came to beg something of you,' Velammal replied.

'Don't beg, command me,' said Madatevan.

242

'My father is getting on in years. He has not very long to live. As long as he lives, let this ruined fort and the spring on the hill belong to him. He is not going to carry these things away with him. Nor will I remain here all by myself; I will away go to live with kinsmen. After that, you can have all this for yourself. I will make no claims. Just be patient for a while!' she said.

'Woman! The fort, the spring, this garden and hut are all yours! I am your slave to command. If you allow me to stay here I will remain, otherwise I will go and enlist in the Company's troops as I did earlier,' said Madatevan.

'Join the white man's troops? Enlist in the army of the demons who hanged Veera Pandya of Panchalankurichi? Don't ever say that again! Stay here. My father has some affection for you. A little meekness on your part will win him over,' Velammal said.

The very next day saw Madatevan try out Velammal's suggestion. He sought Karuppiah Servai and said, 'Mama! I have thought things over. I know I was wrong to quarrel with you. I am an orphan. I have no kith or kin. There is no one living for miles around us. We have no one to rely upon except each other. Why should we fight? I have a suggestion. What do you say to my giving you a fourth of the yield from my land in return for the use of the water which flows through your fort?'

'Tambi! That's the way to talk! Why did you not have the wits to think of this before?' was the old man's triumphant rejoinder.

'Let bygones be bygones, Mama! Let's now think of what has to be done in the future. Why don't you come and take a look at my garden one day?' Madatevan said eagerly.

'Why not? And tell me if you need any help. Both my daughter and I will do what we can. You don't know my daughter. She has very skilful hands,' the old man said.

'Certainly not, Mama! Will I ever ask a man of your age, or your daughter, to work in the garden? I will be satisfied if you merely visit me once in a while. Didn't I tell you I am alone in the world? Your friendship will be the best help I can get!'

The old man and his daughter went to visit Madatevan's garden that very same day. The allotment of a fourth-share in the produce for himself made the old man lose all traces of jealousy. Happy to see how well the garden was maintained, he gave ideas to improve its yield.

'Whatever you may say, I will certainly do some work in the garden. My limbs have not lost all their energy yet. I can weed and water the plants. And once she gets accustomed to it, Velammal can also do a lot of work. It is true that in our caste, women are not used to going out to work. But is it possible to hold on to such customs? Times have changed. Man or woman, we must all find means of survival. It is no shame to work with one's hands.'

Here Madatevan broke in with these words, 'Mama! There is no need at all for your daughter to work in the garden. But it will be a great help if she can save me the trouble of having to cook for myself.'

The old man was delighted. Karuppiah Servai had many times indulged in the same thoughts. All his problems would be solved if only he could get the young man to marry Velammal. Then there would be no need to send Velammal away anywhere. He could spend all his days with her. And instead of a fourth of the yield, all of Madatevan's land would become his to control! Then there would be no one to gainsay him! So ran the thoughts of the greedy old man. But outwardly he spoke with some brusqueness.

'Tambi! Such things are not to be decided so quickly. Everything depends on what Velammal wants. I will never go against her wishes,' said the old man.

Velammal responded only to the explicit meaning of Madatevan's request. 'Appa! This is no great matter. What's so difficult about cooking for three instead of two? Let him come home and eat with you everyday if he likes. It is no problem for me.'

'Why should I object if it's no problem for you?' said old Karuppiah Servai.

245

## 2

For a few days after that, life was all joy for them. There was no satiating Madatevan's eyes, no matter how many times and from how many angles they watched Velammal. It was the same with Velammal. To her eyes, the sky and the earth wore new colours. She floated in the air. She flew in the open skies. She drank from the moonbeams and sported with the stars. The ruined fort became the magnificent palace of the kings. The hill spring appeared a pool of golden lotuses. The velvela tree on its bank was transformed into the celestial karpaka vriksha. Indra and Chandra ran to do her bidding. Rati and Manmatha dressed her in splendour. The jasmine of the woods became the mandara flower of the heavens. Ragi porridge tasted like the nectar of the gods.

An unhappy incident interrupted their idyll. One day the Company troops marched by. An English major headed it on horseback. His greedy eyes fell upon Madatevan's cucumber garden. He signalled with his hand and called out to Madatevan, who was at work on the patch, 'Come here, man, come here!' Guessing what he wanted, Madatevan approached the Major durai.

'Man, any cucumbers to sell? How many per coin?' he asked.

'Durai! There are no cucumbers,' Madatevan replied.

Looking at the garden, the Major said, 'Yes, there are. Why do you lie?'

'I don't lie, sir! They are still tender. Take a week to grow.'

'All the better if they are tender. Pluck ten dozens, fast!'

'It's a sin to pluck them while they are still so tender, sir! All my work will go waste!'

'Damn you! I give the order and you dare to say no! Jamedar! Come here!'

The Jamedar came up to the durai who said something to him. At once the Jamedar rushed into the garden with some fifteen soldiers. They plucked everything in sight, including the flowers and shoots. They also tore off the cucumber creepers, savaging the patches. At first Madatevan thought of trying to restrain them. But he controlled himself because he realized that it was impossible. He watched their brutal actions in a fiery rage.

When the soldiers came out of the ravished garden, Madatevan went up to the Major durai and asked him, 'Sir, is this fair? Will God endure such injustice?'

'Damn your God, man! Have you paid tax to the Company for this cucumber patch?'

'Tax? No one asked me to pay tax, and so I didn't pay it.'

'That is just an excuse. Never mind. I will set off the cucumbers we have plucked against the tax you have to pay,'

247

the Major durai laughed. Many other soldiers laughed with him as they marched on.

When he approached the ruined fort, the Major asked, 'Why hasn't this fort been razed to the ground? Shall we fire our cannon upon it?' The Jamedar replied, 'Waste of gunpowder. There's nothing in this fort except broken walls.'

'Does no one live here?'

'Just an old man and his daughter. He had an old rifle, spear and sword for hunting. We grabbed them from him long ago.'

'Isn't that the old man there? What is his daughter like? Pretty?'

'Yes, as pretty as an orangoutang.' The durai burst into laughter at the Jamedar's reply. In a few minutes the soldiers vanished beyond Arjunan Hill.

For the rest of the day, Karuppiah Servai, Velammal and Madatevan spoke of nothing but the atrocities perpetrated by the Company forces.

'I was with the Company troops for two years,' said Madatevan. 'I left because I couldn't suffer those atrocities.'

'Good thing too. Who will serve these demons?'

'The time has come to put a stop to their atrocities. Only yesterday did I hear that thousands of people gathered together, marched to Palayamkottai prison, tore down its walls, freed Umaidurai and his valiant men. Umaidurai is also collecting a huge army of his own. They have rebuilt the Palayamkottai fort, which had been razed to the ground by the white men's forces. If you two give me leave, I want to join Umaidurai's troops,' the young man said.

Karuppiah Servai was frightened by these words. 'No, not now, Tambi!' he said. 'Let's see how Umaidurai fares. These white men are monsters come out of the underworld. Lord Muruga, who killed Surapadman, must appear again in order to wipe them out. Wait for a while. Let's watch the course of events and then take a decision.'

Later that day, when Velammal met Madatevan alone she said, 'I don't agree with father. We must fight against the Company troops of the white foreigners. Only one thing scares me. My father has a wavering mind. As soon as you leave, he might force me into marriage with someone else. It doesn't matter if you enlist after we are married.'

'You are right. Let's fix the first suitable day to get married. Then we will see what should be done according to the needs of the time,' said Madatevan.

It was essential to fight the foreign men of the Company. But leaving Velammal was not an easy thing to do. Moreover, Madatevan's whole frame burned at the thought of Velammal marrying another. Even the destruction of the cucumber patch did not rouse him to such fury. Therefore he postponed the idea of joining Umaidurai's forces.

## 3

A few days later came even more disheartening news. Wherever people gathered, they talked of the brutal war between the forces of Umaidurai and the Company, the victory of the latter, and the decimation of the Panchalankurichi forces to the very last man. Velammal sobbed and wept over this. Madatevan was stunned. Karuppiah Servai consoled them. But he didn't have to console them for long. Youth is a time of quick recovery from sorrows, especially for lovers. Madatevan and Velammal lost track of the outside world in dreaming of their future together.

Twice or thrice when Madatevan proposed a date for the wedding the old man said, 'Yes, we will fix a date after offering worship to the deity of the clan.'

But came the day when all Madatevan's castles in the air crashed to the ground like the chieftains' forts destroyed by the Company's cannons.

On a shopping trip to Sivagangai to buy some essential goods, Madatevan went to the jewellers' and made enquiries about the gold ornaments he would need to buy as gifts for his bride. Unable to decide on what to buy, he returned home, resolving to take Velammal with him to choose for herself. When he went up to the fort excited by the prospect of talking over this matter, he saw a stranger there. The newcomer was standing against a pillar. Velammal was washing his feet with the hot water she had boiled in a pot. Sitting beside him, Karuppiah Servai was engaged in some conversation with the man.

Madatevan took in the scene from the threshold. No one noticed his coming. He left without being seen.

Madatevan could do no work in the cucumber patch that day. His felt limp, drained of all strength. He kept glancing up at the ruined fort and the spring. Once he caught sight of Velammal going to the spring with a pot in her hand. When he reached the spring, she was about to leave with the filled pot on her waist. Madatevan went and stood before her, as if barring the way.

'What's the matter? Why do you stare at me in this strange way?' she asked.

'Yes, from now onwards I will certainly seem strange to you!' Madatevan said.

'I don't understand what you mean,' said Velammal.

'Of course you won't understand.'

'Never mind. Let me go. I have work to do.'

'Certainly. Am I stopping you?' said Madatevan and stepped aside.

Velammal walked on, but slowed down hesitantly once or twice. Madatevan would not look at her.

She went home muttering angrily under her breath.

That afternoon Madatevan did not go to her home for lunch as he always did. Nor could he engage himself in work. He moved about restlessly and kept babbling to himself.

As the sun sank down in the evening, Velammal came to the garden with a vessel full of rice.

When he saw her, Madatevan began to dig furiously and pretended not to notice her.

Velammal came and stood before him. 'Why didn't you come for lunch?' she asked.

'Didn't want to come. Why are you here?' Madatevan asked.

'I brought food for you. Father asked me to take it to you.'

'I don't want any food. Keep it all for your new guest.'

Velammal was astonished. 'You know that we have a guest?' she asked.

'Why not? Just because you two—father and daughter— are so dazzled by your new guest that you have no eyes for anyone else, did you imagine I would be equally blind?'

'I see! So you do have eyes! All along I had thought you were blind!'

'Yes, I am certainly blind. Otherwise, would I have mistaken an ass for a horse? Worshipped the devil as a goddess?'

'What did you say? Whom do you call ass and devil? You have become crazy. I am leaving the food here. Eat it if you like, or starve to death,' said Velammal and put the vessel down.

'I don't want anything from you. Don't leave the food here. Take it with you and feed any dog you like!' With that, Madatevan kicked the vessel. The pot rolled over and the rice got spilt.

'I will never come here again!' Velammal sobbed as she left the garden.

## 4

From that very night, smoke from the kitchen stove began to rise out of Madatevan's hut. He started cooking for himself as before.

The next day Karuppiah Servai came seeking Madatevan.

'Tambi! Didn't see you the whole of yesterday. Where were you?' he asked.

'I hadn't gone anywhere. You didn't see me, because you have eyes only for your new guest.'

'That is true. It is our duty to care for our guest. And he has arrived with wounds all over his body. Do you know who he is? Did Velammal tell you?'

'Who talked to her?'

'Didn't she tell you? She did bring food for you last evening.'

'She did. But I told her I didn't want it.'

'It was I who told her to bring your food over here for a few days. The newcomer is my sister's son. If he sees you, he will want to know who you are. I thought all that was unnecessary.'

'So the sister's son has made a sudden descent on you after all these years of absence!'

'What is so surprising about that? Everywhere they are enlisting and disbanding men for the armies these days. Today a chieftain is all-supreme. Tomorrow he hangs from the tamarind tree. Didn't you yourself land on us suddenly just two years ago?'

'Why talk of that now? I have work to do. No time for gossip. Go and take care of your guest!'

'Don't be so agitated, Tambi! The guest is a man of wealth. He won't live long. If we take care of him till then, all his wealth will become yours. Then you and Velammal need not have a single care as long as you live.'

'I don't want that kind of wealth. You and your daughter can keep it all! I know how to earn my living with my own hands,' said Madatevan and walked briskly away to work in the patch.

'The boy has gone crazy!' said the old man as he left the garden.

The next four or five days passed without incident. A volcano smoked in Madatevan's heart, ready to spew lava at the earliest opportunity. Such a chance did offer itself soon.

254

One day, happening by chance to look at the spring on top of the hill, Madatevan recalled the many joyful evenings he had spent there with Velammal. He sighed deeply as he remembered the many castles in the air they had built together. His heart ached whenever he thought of those moments. He looked at the spring eagerly, wondering if his grief would be assuaged somewhat if he went to that familiar spot.

A man was standing there. The golden light of the sun sinking behind the hill made him appear like a tall black figure of stone. A little later, a woman's form came and stood beside the tall man. The two figures moved to sit under the velvela tree near the spring. Madatevan's heart began to seethe. All his suppressed fury boiled over. He leapt to the top of the hill in a turbulent rage. But the woman was no longer there. Only the man sat there, leaning against the velvela tree. With his eyes eagerly scanning the west, he remained unaware of Madatevan's arrival.

Madatevan had been fencing the garden. So he had some coir rope with him, as also a knife stuck at the waist. When he saw the man all alone, something flashed in his head. He went behind him, threw the rope around him and bound him to the tree. Then he came forward with the knife in his hand. 'You scoundrel! Blackguard! Who are you? Tell me why you are here. How dare you come between Velammal and me? We were inseparable, about to get married. Our

255

hearts beat as one. You came and ruined our lives. Why did you come? What's in your mind? Confess the truth. Swear to me that you will leave right away without seeing her again. If you do that, I will forgive you and let you go. Otherwise I will kill you with this knife. That's for sure. Will you or won't you give me this promise?'

The man bound thus said not a word but gazed at Madatevan with intense surprise. His lips moved once as if about to speak, but no word came out.

'Why are you blinking at me like a thief caught stealing sheep? Why don't you answer? I won't kill you when you are bound to the tree. If you are ready for a sword fight, I will release you. But don't think you can escape by running away. Don't imagine you can hide in the fort either. I know every corner, I know all the secret paths of the fort. I will smoke you out of any hiding place,' Madatevan roared.

Still, the bound man stayed silent.

Madatevan's rage knew no bounds. 'Can't you speak? Are you dumb?'

The face that had reflected only surprise so far, now broke into a smile. It was a strange smile. Madatevan could make nothing of it. His anger mounted.

'Why do you smile? Are you laughing at me? Are you making fun of me? Look! I will kill you with a single stroke. That is the right punishment for the man who snatched my beloved from me!' So saying Madatevan raised his knife.

The bound man's glance was directed at something behind Madatevan. At the same time came the sounds of running footsteps.

Velammal's frightened accents were heard, 'You wretch! Stop! Stop! Do you know what you are doing?' Madatevan looked back. His smouldering heart flamed forth.

'Wretch, am I? What about you who forgot all your vows and betrayed me? I will first kill you and then kill your lover!' Madatevan screamed and aimed his knife at Velammal.

'Ayyo!' as Velammal shrieked something crackled behind Madatevan. Before he could turn back, the hand holding the knife was in the grip of another. The next instant, his other hand was similarly grabbed. It was no ordinary grip; the iron grip was by hands of steel. From head to foot, Madatevan felt his nerves tauten to breaking point. His body trembled visibly.

Madatevan craned his neck and looked behind him. The coir ropes round the tree were shredded to pieces. The man who had freed himself from the knots wore the same strange smile as before.

Madatevan's lips quivered.

'Blockhead! Don't you see who it is? Don't you have any brains in your head? Eyes in your face?' Velammal screamed.

At once something flashed in Madatevan's mind. It filled his head with a message from the skies. His whole body thrilled to an ecstasy sublime. His taut nerves relaxed once again. The knife in his hand slipped to the ground.

At once the iron hands relaxed their grip.

'Velamma? Is this Umaidurai himself?' Madatevan asked.

'And you didn't know it all this while! How smart you are!' said Velammal.

'Sami! Durai!' Madatevan stretched himself on the ground before the man and grabbed his feet. 'Forgive me for the wrong I did in ignorance. It is said that God himself seeks his devotees out. You came seeking me even before I went in search of you. Durai! My love for this wretched woman blinded my eyes. Shouldn't she have informed me earlier? She too betrayed me!'

Umaidurai smiled again. Then he stammered out these words. ' T-t-tambi! S-see this s-s-urul vaal? I h-h-ave s-s-liced off s-s-even heads in a s-s-ingle f-f-ling. D-do you s-s-still want m-me t-t-to f-f-ight you?' With that, Umaidurai pulled out the surul vaal and flung it in the air. The blades on each side flashed as the weapon swooped through the air like lightning, for about sixteen feet, and returned to the owner's hand. It hissed like a cobra as it fanned out in flight.

'Sami! I am not afraid of your surul vaal. If the same weapon were in the hands of the enemy, I would see what I could do with my little folding knife. But how can I fight you? I longed to see you at least once in my lifetime. I was broken-hearted to hear that you had died on the battlefield. But now I am filled with a new life. I will do my utmost to obey any command of yours. I am ready to place myself, my life and all that I possess at your feet. Try me!'

Umaidurai's eyes became moist. Velammal too shed tears of joy. The three of them returned to the fort.

## 5

Madatevan had taken permission to reserve a room for himself in the fort, to store those odds and ends not in immediate use, or so he told Karuppiah Servai. He unlocked it for Umaidurai to see. The room had some boxes and bundles in sacks, all containing black explosives. Rifles, spears and swords were piled beside them. 'Sami! I have collected all these things for you. Tell me how to use them,' said Madatevan.

Madatevan was very busy for the next week. He went to several places carrying secret messages from Umaidurai for various men. Finally, Umaidurai entrusted the young man with a very important task. He was to go to Sivagangai and discover the whereabouts of Chinna Marudu Servai. Then he was to see China Marudu and inform him that Umaidurai was alive, but without disclosing his hiding place. He was to evaluate Marudu's bent of mind, and he was to ask the man if he was ready to join forces with Umaidurai in utterly destroying the white weed which was poisoning the country. Umaidurai repeated this last message several times. Madatevan understood it thoroughly and set out with zeal.

At Sivagangai, he learnt that Chinna Marudu Servai was living in a manor he had built at a place called Siruvayal. Reaching Siruvayal, he secured a meeting with Chinna Marudu and found that the chieftain was extremely happy to know that Umaidurai was still alive. He sent word back that Umaidurai should come immediately to his Siruvayal manor, from where he could gather a force of twenty thousand men within fifteen days. Under the leadership of a great warrior like Umaidurai, they were sure to be able to wipe out all traces of white men from the country.

It was with this heartening message that Madatevan began his return journey to the ruined fort as swiftly as he could. But on the way, he faced a hurdle. He did not succeed in trying to get unobtrusively past a small platoon of the East India Company. Some soldiers captured him and took him to into the central tent where they were quartered. There, they bound him to a pole.

That was when he happened to overhear a conversation from the adjacent tent. An old voice declared, 'I know where Umaidurai is hiding. I can take you to him.' The same voice also asked for payment of the five-thousand-rupee award that the Company had announced for such information.

'Oh yes, the reward will be given after Umaidurai is captured,' said the Major durai, and added, 'Jamedar! For the moment, give this old man a strong dose of some old liquor.' So spoke the major's voice.

'Don't send a large contingent; then he will escape. Send four or five brave-hearted men with me. If I don't catch him for you, change my name to _____!' said the old man.

Madatevan was tortured by this conversation. Unable to break free from his bonds, he was in despair. Just then the Major durai entered his tent.

'Oh, I know this young man! Didn't we get a whole lot of cucumbers from his garden?' said the Major.

'Yes, yajaman! Don't know why they have captured me,' Madatevan said.

'What, man! Why don't you join the Company troops? You'll get a good salary.'

'Yajaman! I was in the army of the Nawab of Arcot. They said I was unfit to fight and sent me away. What is the use of joining now? I will plant cucumbers and get a good crop ready, to give you when you pass that way. Thousands will be lured by the salary to join the Company's forces. But can everyone grow cucumber?' asked Madatevan.

261

The Major was well pleased with that answer. 'You are right. Grow a good crop of cucumbers. Next time I won't take it in lieu of taxes. I will buy them at the rate of four cucumbers per coin!' said he.

At the Major's orders, Madatevan was set free. Thanking the durai with folded hands, Madatevan made his way out and rushed as fast as he could back to the ruined fort.

## 6

As Madatevan approached Arjunan Hill, he saw Umaidurai and Velammal sitting on the broken wall of the fort, eagerly watching out for him. He didn't wait for their enquiries.

'Sami! I have good news for you. Chinna Maruda Servai asked me to tell you to go to him at once. You must leave this instant. There must be no delay. Velamma! Sami must not go alone. You must accompany him up to Siruvayal,' said Madatevan.

Velammal, who did not know the reason for such haste, looked at Umaidurai in perplexity. Once again a smile creased Umaidurai's face. He jumped up to leave at once.

'S-s-she n-need n-not c-come. I will g-g-go b-by m-myself. I kn-now th-the way,' he said.

'Please, durai! I beg you; you must definitely take her with you. Velamma! Why do you hesitate? I see you haven't

262

understood the matter. On the way, I saw the company's troops. They will be here very soon. Take sami by the short-cut up to Siruvayal and come back.'

Then Velammal knew the reason for his agitation. And yet she hung back.

'What will you and father do?' she asked.

'I will save myself. God will take care of your father. I swear it on Lord Murugan! Go at once!' he said.

Both got ready to leave.·

'Wait, sami!' Madatevan, and ran into the fort. He was back as swiftly with a gun in his hand. 'Take it with you,' he said.

Umaidurai shrugged. He threw the surul vaal once again. 'Th-this is en-nough f-for m-m-me, you k-keep it,' he said and left.

Umaidurai and Velammal walked away. As they were about to round the hill and disappear from view, Velammal bounded back and flung her arms around Madatevan's neck.

'You suspected me. Now you are sending me away with sami!' she said.

'Is this the time to talk of suspicions?' Madatevan tried to divert her.

'But I suspect you,' said Velammal.

'What madness is this?' asked Madatevan.

263

'You are asking me to go in order to save my life, aren't you?'

'Take it that way if you like. Don't I have a right over your life?'

'Yes, you have that right in all our subsequent births. Therefore you must swear to remain alive until I return. I will go only if you swear it.'

'Woman! I swear it. Lord Murugan has to be responsible for my word.'

'Don't you worry, I will pray to Murugan.' With those words, Velammal looked at Madatevan as if she would consume him with her eyes. Then she withdrew her arms and ran away.

Madatevan went to his hut. He took some weapons and a few other things out. Then he set fire to the roof of the hut. When the hut started burning, he went up to the fort. He found a convenient spot on its wall to wait with a gun in his hand.

In a little while, the light from the burning hut revealed the approach of seven or eight men on the highway. They stood talking beside the burning hut. Then four men from the group came forward.

Madatevan pulled the trigger. The shot was fired with a bang. All four men jumped aside. No one was hurt. A second and third round fared no better.

The men talked together. One of them returned the way he came. The rest sat on the highway, out of range of gunshot.

Suddenly one of them made a rush towards the fort shouting, 'Velamma! My daughter!'

Madatevan could make out that it was Karuppiah Servai. When he had been in the Company tent, the voice he heard from the adjacent tent had been Servai's. But why was he rushing towards the fort with a scream? Was it some kind of a trap? For a second, Madatevan thought of shooting at the traitor. But there was no need. One of the men at the back was before him. The old man fell with a screech. 'The traitor is justly punished.' The thought made Madatevan happy. How lucky that Velammal remained ignorant of his treachery! What anguish she would suffer if she knew!

It was not as big an achievement to have warned Umaidurai and sent him to safety before the danger came. What a good idea to have sent Velammal away under the pretext of guiding his path!

Until then Madatevan's efforts had borne fruit. Only, he didn't know how to proceed after that. He had thought that the men would enter the fort and that he would have a free hand in deciding their fate. But they seemed determined to stay away, no doubt deterred by the belief that Umaidurai was still within the fort. Well and good! The longer they waited, the more time Umaidurai would have to reach Siruvayal. Let these blockheads wait here! Let them think of Umaidurai's surul vaal and die of fear!

The waiting competition continued till midnight. Madatevan's eyes began to close. After all, he was still a young man. Suddenly he saw a row of black ants moving along the highway from the north.

No, no! They were not black ants. It was the army of the British company. Good God! How vast it was! Two hundred, four hundred, a thousand men? What can I do against so huge an army? Yet I must do something memorable. When the company troops entered Panchalankurichi, didn't every warrior within the fort put an end to many, many lives? I must do the same and enter the warriors' heaven. But poor Velamma! What about the promise I made to her? What is the use of thinking about it now? Hasn't she placed her trust in Lord Murugan? Let Murugan take care of it. Why should I worry?

As Madatevan was cogitating thus, the company troops advanced closer. What's that? A long vehicle on wheels in the middle of the troops? What does the cart carry?

The advance guard stood exactly where the men who had come earlier had waited. Some confabulations took place. The soldiers near the long cart were engaged in some task. I see! It is a cannon! Have they filled it with powder?

266

Madatevan was rather stunned. He had not expected the arrival of a cannon or that it would open fire to utterly raze the fort to the ground. But it would not be necessary to waste too much gunpowder. The cannon had an easy task before it. Hadn't Madatevan collected bundles and bundles of gunpowder by stealth and stored them in the fort? If that room received a single shot, the entire fort would be destroyed at once. Madatevan would also meet the same fate. Velamma! You did well to put your faith in Murugan! But what can Murugan do about the cannonade of the Company troops?

The reason for the old man's panic became obvious. He must have been sick with fear for his daughter when he learnt of the plan to use cannon fire to destroy the fort.

The hut had burnt itself out. There was blackness everywhere. Tearing out of the darkness, a lightning flashed at the mouth of the cannon. The next instant, a terrifying explosion was heard. It was enough to cause a tremor in the walls of the fort. The cannon ball burst into the fort. The noise was that of a thousand cracks of thunder sounding in unison. Next came an endless flare of flame. Then the skies crashed in with a deafening clamour. The hill and the fort came tumbling down. Madatevan rolled down. As he fell, he lost consciousness.

When Madatevan came to, he felt an excruciating pain

267

shooting through his leg. He found himself struggling for breath. He was drenched with sweat all over. It was pitch dark. He had never experienced such darkness before. He wondered if he had gone blind. No, his eyes were all right. He moved his hands—ice cold rock on both sides and above him. The ground at his feet was all stones and earth. He couldn't move an inch forward or backward. Something pressed hard upon his leg preventing it from moving. It caused unbearable pain.

He could hear voices as if from some underworld.

'See, Umaidurai has once again slipped out of the net!'

'We have searched everywhere. There is no place left to search.'

'He must have slunk away even before the cannon was brought in.'

'People are right to call Umaidurai a sorcerer.'

'He can't escape forever. We will send troops to search everywhere.'

'He must have made it to Sivagangai.'

'No, he must be at the Kamudi Fort.'

'Or he might be hiding in the forest.'

'Did the old drunk deceive us or was he himself deceived?'

'Idiots! Why did you shoot him dead? He should have been hung as an example to others.'

Madatevan felt some glee in visualizing the old man

hanging from a tree. It would have been just punishment
for that scoundrel and traitor. But how painful for Velammal
if she were to see it! Velamma! Velamma! I am not going to
see you again. I feel faint. My life is ebbing away.

## 7

Life had a strong hold on Madatevan, as he realized when
he recovered consciousness again. He could also see dimly.
He tried hard to see where he was. He realized that a part
of the fort's masonry had made an awkward descent on him.
His head and body had escaped being crushed only because
another stone by the side had propped it up. But a huge
rock must have fallen on his leg. The bone must be broken.
Otherwise, would the pain be so unbearable?

As time passed, the rocks beside him began to warm up
under the sun. The heat increased. His mouth was parched
with thirst. He began to feel the pangs of hunger. Did he
have to die like this, agonized by hunger and thirst? Why
hadn't the wall fallen over his head and killed him
instantaneously? Muruga! Is this the return for Velammal's
prayers?

From somewhere at a great distance and from a cave
under the depths of the earth, came a faint voice shouting,
'Muruga! Muruga!'

'Muruga! Where is my affianced husband? Where is the

man I love? Where is my darling whom I entrusted to your care?' came the very, very faint but clear voice of lament.

Madatevan tried to respond to it. 'Velamma!' he called. But he himself could not hear his own voice. How would Velammal hear it? Ayyo! Muruga! Will Velammal leave without discovering me as the Company soldiers did?

No! Murugan could not be so cruel. Velammal is coming closer. I can hear her voice more clearly. Gathering all his strength, Madatevan shouted, 'Velamma!'

'My darling!' Velammal screamed as she came running. With a tremendous effort, somehow she managed to push aside the rock that lay on his leg. Even before recovering from that breathless effort, she grabbed his legs and pulled him out from under the debris.

'Wretch! My leg is broken! The pain is killing me! Don't touch! Don't pull me!'

As soon as Madatevan came out from under the rocks, Velammal fell upon him and wept with her arms around him in an embrace. Pushing her back forcibly, Madatevan indicated with a gesture that he was thirsty. At once Velammal carried him to the spring. Only when she poured water into his mouth with her cupped hands did Madatevan feel his life return.

'Velamma! See how I kept my word to you? I have lost my leg though,' he said. Velammal sobbed as she looked at his leg.

270

'Don't weep for me, Velamma! Weep for your father. I am still alive though I have lost my leg. But he is dead and gone. But why weep for him? We must not cry over one who died a warrior's death. If only you had seen your father standing beside me and fighting the company troops. Why, even Veera Pandian and Umaidurai would have been astounded!'

Velammal stopped crying to ask, 'Was my father really on your side? I had other suspicions.'

'Other suspicions? And you were the one who was mad at me for harbouring suspicions. All suspicion is evil.'

'True, I shouldn't have had those suspicions. A little while ago I suspected even Murugan. But Murugan saved your life for me,' said Velammal.

Murugan's grace and Velammal's nursing made Madatevan recover. But the leg was lost forever. He had to lead his life as a disabled man.

Velammal was not at all unhappy about marrying a man without a leg. In fact, she was proud of it. She herself grew cucumbers in the garden, sold the crop and ran her home, taking every care of her husband.

For seven years, they lived together in joy. Then Madatevan passed away.

As long as he lived, he never disclosed the old man's treachery to Velammal, but continued to tell her that he

271

had died battling against the Company's troops.

Velammal, too, kept her secret safe until she died. On the night Madatevan had sent her to guide Umaidurai on his way, she had taken her leave of Umaidurai in a little while and returned to the fort. From behind the tree near the spring, she had witnessed everything that took place. She also saw her father's act of treachery. But she never referred to it. If she did, how could she explain how she came by that knowledge? Wouldn't she have to admit that she had abandoned Umaidurai along the way?

Coming to know of the life of this remarkable couple, people from the villages near by placed a memorial stone for Madatevan beside the spring. They also planted a spear beside it for Lord Murugan who protected him. In course of time, the spring came to be called Madatevan's Spring.

Even today, villagers who pass by fold their hands reverently before the memorial stone and spear, and make an offering to them of the flowers from the oleander plant beside the spring.

# Translator's Notes

The stories in this collection have been chosen to represent the variety of concerns that impelled Kalki to write. Most of them are charged by Gandhian ideals and social consciousness. Some explore the human mind with its tangle of predictable and unpredictable responses and motivations. You will find many tones here from satire to romance, pathos to fantasy, and also, repeatedly, the fervour of patriotism. The strong and the meek find a place, as do the upright and the corrupt. Some of the women characters show surprising facets. An undercurrent of humour runs through the whole, sometimes bright, at other times grim.

Most of these stories, written over a long period of time (1925–1950) have been reprinted several times during the author's life and after. You can trace the growth of the writer's art across them. I shall take a leaf out of Kalki's own book, and chat with you about the whats and the whys of each story in these notes.

No translator can ever be satisfied with his/her effort. Even A.K. Ramanujan, that greatest of all Indian translators, remarked that, unlike a piece of creative writing, you could never say you have completed a translation. The first effort is only the first step. You go on making changes, editing, inserting, cutting, in short, working on your translation through your life. My translations began as an effort to introduce Kalki to my daughter and son, both of whom are unable to read him in the original. I began by reading some stories aloud to them in Tamil; I then translated a few more for them to read by themselves. This has therefore been a work done sporadically, over the last five or six years. My language changed to suit my two auditors, as they grew older. I also think I got better at my job as I went along, certainly more daring as I gained experience. In the process I realized that I had to be faithful to the mood and not so much to the word. Finding the balance between the two is the acid test for all translators.

This book is really only a scratching of the surface. I would be delighted if others were to see it as a beginning of the task of translating more and more from the massive oeuvre of both the fiction and non-fiction of Kalki R. Krishnamurthy. It would not only introduce a writer of substance to non-Tamils, but also provide researchers with a treasure trove of material in studying the socio-political currents of the significant pre-Independence period in which he lived. I have succeeded to an extent with my children. I have aroused in them a more than casual interest in Kalki's writings. And I would be very happy if I succeed in doing that with you!

## THE LETTER

Kalki believed that women were the equals of men. They had the right to education and liberation. He opposed the atrocities perpetuated by orthodox society upon widows in two of his most moving short stories. He incurred the wrath of the hidebound when he wrote his novel *Tyagabhumi* (1939), where his provocatively-named woman protagonist Savitri refuses to obey a court order which compels her to return to a tyrannical husband. She is willing to pay alimony to keep him at bay. Urged to give in for the sake of traditional ideals of Indian womanhood, she responds angrily, 'I will make any sacrifice for freedom, but none for slavery.' Rousing scenes like this were roundly condemned when they appeared in print, and launched a raging controversy around a film based on the novel.

'The Letter' was the author's tribute to a real-life protagonist who dedicated herself to the cause of women's emancipation. The events in the story are fictitious, but the protagonist Annapurani Devi was modelled after Sister Subbulakshmi (1886–1969) who founded the Vidhavashram (Home for Widows) and Sarada Vidyalayam, an educational institution for women. Herself a child-widow, she worked tirelessly for women's welfare.

The author's admiration for Sister Subbulakshmi's contribution was evident in the glowing tribute he paid her in a special article in his magazine, and in the reverent tone he adopts to describe Annapurani Devi. The fictional character becomes wholly credible because of the real-life 'heroine'.

A postscript in Kalki's biography describes how the author chanced on the idea for the story while on holiday in Tirunelveli. Walking over the bridge across the river Tamraparani, he suddenly hit upon the opening of the narrative, discussed it with a young colleague, and told him the entire story.

Tradition finds its new avatar here with the use of the nadaswaram, and its auspiciousness is defined anew.

## THE POISON CURE

'The Poison Cure' is one of Kalki's earliest stories. It deals with a problem that is alive and rampant in India after fifty years of independence and democracy.

276

The young Krishnamurthy sounds confident, believing fervently that the success of the freedom movement would automatically put an end to such social evils. Rational means of persuasion are seemingly sufficient to convince the die-hards that they are wrong, and to convert them into worthy citizens of a brave new world. The young narrator in the story, apprehensive about winning his case, is the author himself. With what excitement he sings the verses of the poet Subrahmania Bharati, whom he read for the first time at age ten, and who remained a life-long source of inspiration to the writer!

The postmaster in the story is none other than Kalki's first teacher in his village school, for whom he had genuine respect, and with whom he always remained a favourite. All that Kalki says about the postmaster, including his bhajanai sessions, the distribution of snacks for children, the curing of victims of snakebite, the veneration for Gandhi, comes from the real-life Ayyasami Ayyar, who introduced Kalki to the frenzied lyrics of Bharati. But when Ayyasami Ayyar read this story, he was not happy. He expressed his grievance that his former pupil had portrayed him as a character who believed in untouchability. Kalki could not convince him that he meant it as a compliment!

## THE REBIRTH OF SRIKANTHAN

The author depicts a woman's strength of mind while flaying a pusillanimous male character. Kalki's language delineates the narrow-minded brahmin household with the knowledge of personal experience. The traditional women speak with an expression of contempt on their faces for the woman who dared to appear on a public platform and address a crowd.

The satire is dependent on the way the language is used to reflect its cultural matrix. At the very start, we are told that Srikanthan was indubitably the male heir of a well-to-do family, there was nothing to suggest the girl in him. Kalki plays throughout on this idea of manliness, usually associated with strength, courage and resolution. In the story, the person who possesses these qualities is a woman. The 'manly' hero turns out to be an utter coward. This familiar theme is given special resonance by the background. The Gandhi-Irwin accord, the failure of the Second Round Table Conference, and the satyagraha which followed, are inextricable links in the tale of love and misplaced trust. The discords of the old father's violin practice at seasonal and unseasonal hours is a subtle motif, moving from humour to pathos and reflecting the essential loneliness of the father and daughter.

A non-Tamil writer wrote after reading this story, 'I don't

278

understand the hero of this story. He baffles me. So I have started looking for the Freud in him. Was Srikanthan (1) mother-fixated? (2) having troubles with women? (3) impotent? Nothing is clear. But that is perhaps the strength of the story. It makes you think, and wonder about the author's intention.'

What made the story of Srikanthan a must for this collection is the complex web of emotions it arouses, which belies its apparent simplicity.

## THE GOVERNOR'S VISIT

A few years ago I happened to be looking at M.F. Husain's series of paintings on the British Raj. One of them arrested my attention. Surely, surely I had seen it before? Where? When? The thought tantalized me. The canvas showed a scene at a railway station of the British days, with a lordly British functionary alighting on the platform and being received, with a sweeping-to-the-ground bow, by an Indian Raja in full royal regalia.

Much later I realized that it was not the painting that I had seen before. I knew all the implications of that bow from Kalki's 'The Governor's Visit'. The furore the news causes is the subject of Kalki's biting pen here. The caricatures are true to life—as anyone who has followed Tamil politics will know. All (s)he has to do is to recall a much-publicized photograph of a State Minister falling full-length at the feet of the then chief minister Jayalalitha Jayaraman in public.

No, things haven't changed much from Kalki's days. Not at all. Servility seems to have become a national trait. The swishing of hands going up and down in endless salaams continues to be a characteristic of our times.

## RURAL FANTASY

Translating 'Rural Fantasy' was a chastening experience because the motifs, behaviour and speech patterns are rooted in the inflexions of the language. There are no descriptive details of the location. The author takes it for granted that his readers will recognize it at once and without any difficulty. That is the advantage of writing for one's own language group. Yet the story seems to move on a cinema screen rather than on the printed page. The author invites you to watch the footage, not up close, but from the balcony seat reserved for you, his dear friend, right next to him, and view the scenes from an objective, tongue-in-cheek distance. He wants you to chuckle and chortle with him over the midsummer madness which has suddenly infected the sleepy, remote village, where, until now, every single day has never failed to be exactly the same as the previous one. And like cinema and television, the style manipulates the response. The 'modern' young woman of the story shocks no more. She

280

has been succeeded by the postmodern woman of a blasé and globalized age. But we know that is not what the story is about. The self-absorption of Kanayazhi is not an isolated phenomenon. Any progress seems transient, superficial. After all the laughter, we are ill-prepared for the image of the garbage—a terrifying visual of stench, filth and disease. It is also an uncharacteristic moment for Kalki. He is forced to admit hopelessness in the face of the general apathy he sees around him, which he despairs of being able to overcome, even in the brave new world of independent India.

## THE TIGER KING

'The Tiger King' is a perennial favourite even though it seems the most dated story in this collection. Maharajas and dewans are no more, the British have left us long ago, we have forgotten shikars and durbars. Tiger hunts are things of the past: there are fewer tigers left in the whole nation than in the kingdom of the Raja in this story. But the tale is such great fun from start to finish! Kalki seems to draw his jokes from an unending source. He revitalizes old jokes in striking new contexts.

A contemporary playwright from Nagpur comments, 'I loved, simply loved, "The Tiger King". I couldn't stop tittering while I read it. The humour springs from the pages. And what a poker face the writer maintains while he narrates the sequence of events! This story will never become stale. Its humour will keep it alive.' I was delighted to find a kindred response.

This frequently is also understandably the most frequently translated of all Kalki's short stories. The German translation was the title story of an anthology of Indian tales, *Der Tiger Konig*, published in 1966.

## Sivakozhundu of Tiruvazhundur

'Sivakozhundu of Tiruvazhundur' is narrated by Kandappa Pillai, a great percussionist. He tells us about a nadaswaram genius who retired from the limelight at the peak of his career.

Several things make this story stand out for me. A mellow music pervades the entire account, rising into a glorious finale of tranquil bliss where the artist has stopped performing for others. But he scales new heights playing for himself. As Kandappa Pillai tells it, listening to the blind, reclusive artist is to experience a vision sublime. Music becomes both image and metaphor for the characters, the narrator and listener. The lovers are at first attracted and finally united by their involvement in their art.

The author knew the ambience of the period and its world of artists at first hand, and paints it with the ease of familiarity. The non-Tamil reader may feel the absence of concrete details to help visualize the scenes and characters.

But Kalki could afford to ignore this and get on with his story, knowing fully well that his readers would know exactly how a street and marketplace in Kumbakonam looked; a nadaswaram party playing at temple festivals was an everyday sight in any part of the state for them. If Sivakozhundu was asked to sit down in Vanaja's house, they knew that it would be on a jamakkalam spread on the ground. They knew that the chokra boy carried the paan box, and ran errands for the artists.

It is the way in which the Gandhian motif is introduced and developed which makes this story unique. Kalki does it so cannily, almost casually, that one is nearly persuaded into thinking it a frill. In the end, it is the Gandhian ideal which pervades the story: a quest for truth in life and in art.

## THE BIG SWELLING SEA

Under the influence of Gandhi and his own beloved mentor Rajaji, Kalki was convinced that violence bred evil, even when directed towards a noble goal. In this story, he condemns terrorism as a means of attaining national freedom, but one can see also see his sneaking admiration for the relentless courage of the terrorists.

Kuttralam, the location, was a favoured locale with Kalki, because it was home to T.K. Chidambaranatha Mudaliar, his dear friend and literary guru, with whom he spent the few holidays he could snatch. There he walked up the hill, bathed in the falls, and listened to TKC recite and expound on old Tamil poetry through the day. Sometimes Rajaji joined them in these literary revels. The places and paths described here were the happy haunts of the three friends.

For me, this was the toughest story to translate. There are two narrative voices, and a double lens to examine the events of the past. Try as I would, the main narrator would not come alive for me. I could not conjure up a picture of the man who betrayed the terrorists, could get no insight into his feelings; even his avarice was not credible.

The story is long and has too many repetitive phrases. The structure is stilted, carelessly crafted. It leaves too many loose ends. The suspense does not bear up to scrutiny. The language evokes few regional flavours, except in the initial passage where the woman is overheard, which the narrator himself singles out as chaste and sweet. It also differs in temperament from the other stories in this collection.

Usually, when Kalki uses an image at a crucial moment, it resonates with meaning. In this story, the final image of the wig and beard floating on the waters remains unexplained. Why had the traitor hoarded them for years? Why did he throw them away, and why at this precise moment? Was he released from some curse—like characters in folk tales and legends—who must tell their tale to break free?

My reason for including it in this collection is quite simple. My children were devouring the adventures of secret societies at that time and I wanted them to read one written by their great-grandfather. I also thought they should know something about Tamil history. Their school lessons taught them about Shaheed Bhagat Singh; but they knew nothing about young Vanchi Iyer who shot himself after shooting Collector Ashe at Maniyachi Junction, or Nilakantha Brahmachari, or even Aurobindo at the Pondicherry Ashram. This is the only story in this collection which has been abridged slightly.

## THE S.S. MENAKA

'The S. S. Menaka' possesses a compelling charm, perhaps more for the central image, rather than the narrative itself: a little lifeboat in the black sea with the full moon above, the sheer beauty of the seascape with the waves swelling and roaring around the reunited lovers. I could not translate the song they sing, an old familiar 'vennila kanni' (a form in which the lyric is addressed to the moon) with its associations with folk music and mysticism, immediately after they witness the horrendous destruction of a ship full of refugees, aware that their little craft may be destroyed at any time, and that they may die of starvation and thirst, abandoned in the ocean.

Though the evacuation of Burma in World War II forms the backdrop, Kalki's story is not about wars and destruction. That is why the major rasa in the story is not bhayanaka but adbhuta: wonder at the ethereal beauty of the physical world, and the possibility of love binding hearts amidst the horror of destruction.

Rajani's life as a prostitute adds to the pathos of the story. It has its own equivalent in an olfactory image—the fragrance from the perfume bottle that the woman uses now and then, to freshen up in the midst of the unspeakable stench and filth. That whiff of perfume establishes her courage and indomitable spirit, qualities which Kalki admired, and thought essential for human existence.

## THE RUINED FORT

Recently, a woman in her seventies quoted whole passages from this story to me and said it had been a favourite when she was young. Neither she nor anyone else seems to have realized that 'The Ruined Fort' is no romantic fiction but a parody of the popular Tamil gothic of Kalki's time. So far, no academic paper or critical text has analysed or identified the model. Kalki's sense of humour invariably coloured his style, triggering experiments with all its streams from farce to satire. He revelled in parody, and was very good at mimicking contemporary writers. He also enjoyed other people's efforts at parody, particularly when he was himself the target.

Parodies turn into straightforward narratives in translation. But this story works because the market continues to be flooded with maudlin romances set in exotic locations. Nor have bodiless spirits ceased to wander through pulp fiction, still paradoxically accessible to living beings through sense perception.

I suspect that Kalki was also indulging in some self-parody here, having set his own novellas *Mohini Teevu* and *Solaimalai Ilavarasi* in just such ruined monuments. The twist at the end is wry enough. No, the writer has no sympathy for those who opt for escapism over action.

## Veenai Bhavani

We are in a different world altogether with 'Veenai Bhavani', more passionate, intense, troubled and painful. The author experiments with melodrama, avoiding its excesses through the filter of the narrative voice. (It is good to remember here that the word melodrama combines the word *melos* or music with drama.) The theme may be passé now but the story holds our attention with its humanism and lyricism. The story has been dramatized on stage and adapted for the radio.

Despite references to the devadasi system, there is no zeal for social reform. The story's roots are unmistakably in the over-two-thousand-year-old akam tradition of Tamil Nadu, the interior landscape that we encounter in the Sangam lyrics. But the later bhakti tradition also makes itself felt in the divine music of the protagonist. Some of the most moving moments in the story are the descriptions of the impact of that music. They could not have been written by anyone who was not himself a musician. Kandappa Pillai understands the craft so well that he fully grasps the inspiration that transcends technique. Kalki's personal passion for the music that he writes about with such feeling is clearly evident.

Interestingly 'Veenai Bhavani' received an immediate letter of appreciation from the then-editor of the Tamil daily *Dinamani*, who said that it was a marvellous story with lasting value, to be savoured by repeated reading. But the associate editor of the same daily wrote a scathing critique of the story in his column in which he charged the author with plagiarism. The author was deluged with letters from readers who pointed to the strange occurrence of the editor and the associate editor of the same daily expressing contrary opinions, and in print. In his reply, Kalki said that the truest criticism came from thousands of readers, and that he was not going to make the editor of the *Dinamani* responsible for the opinions expressed by his critic.

He added that a story like 'Veenai Bhavani' could have been born only in the cultural milieu of Tamil Nadu.

Recent criticism has found fault with the story's conclusion because the central character Bhavani is pushed into the wings and the focus is on Kandappa Pillai, the narrator. I see this as an advantage. It re-establishes a sense of perspective which we were in danger of losing through the tides of emotion. Secondly, it gives depth to the narration. Only a man as wise as Kandappa Pillai could have understood the passions which raged in the hearts of the lovers, and depicted them with such sympathy. And maintained that delicate balance between his attachment for them and the detachment which enabled him to weigh the consequences carefully before he acted.

## MADATEVAN'S SPRING

When Kalki wrote this story for the special Deepavali issue of his magazine in 1950, he had been acclaimed as the greatest exponent of the historical romance in Tamil. This long story gives you a taste of his approach to the genre. Neither language nor style can by themselves create a sense of the past in fiction; a certain sensibility is needed, as we see in 'Madatevan's Spring'.

Kalki does not change his language either in narration

or dialogue. He uses other means to evoke a historic past. The chieftains of the times, who fought against the British East India Company and died in the battlefield, were familiar to his readers through legends and ballads. Kalki makes them come alive as the heroes of his protagonists. Veera Pandya Kattabomman has been hanged before the story starts; there is only a reference to Chinna Marudu Servai. But they are already inspiring figures for the people. Kattabomman's brother Umaidurai (literally, the Dumb Lord) appears briefly, but leaves an indelible impression of valour and skill at arms. His invincible spirit illumines the story.

A recent study of the story points out how the historical account of Umaidurai's having received shelter and succour from a woman in a time of danger, is used by the author to strengthen his tale. His fictional Velammal plays that historical role, straining neither accuracy or credibility. Likewise, Madatevan's memory of the fate of the Panchalankurichi fort, where the warriors died to the last man, buttresses the resolution of the fictional character with its historical resonance.

The incident of the cucumber patch is drawn directly from an old satirical ballad: 'Somewhere, in some garden, someone grew cucumbers. The white man sent him a letter ordering that he should sell two cucumbers per coin.' Kalki's readers would have laughed at this clever stroke, especially as the satire is valid in contemporary times.

The references to Murugan, a special god in popular Tamil cosmology, are particularly apt in the context of the time, place and social milieu. This is borne out in the story by the tradition of the veerakal (memorial stone) with Murugan's vel (spear) beside it.

Though Kalki admired physical courage, he does not permit the use of Madatevan's secret cache of explosives in the destruction of human life. Madatevan's shots miss their target as well. Ultimately it is tender love, fierce patriotism, and pride in making sacrifices in the cause of freedom which emerge as the lauded ideals in this story, triumphing over evil and treachery, as Gandhi believed they did, and as Kalki dreamed they would.